Charlotte Mary Yonge

Lady Hester

Outlook

Charlotte Mary Yonge

Lady Hester

1. Auflage | ISBN: 978-3-73261-914-6

Erscheinungsort: Paderborn, Deutschland

Erscheinungsjahr: 2018

Outlook Verlag GmbH, Paderborn.

Charlotte Mary Yonge

Lady Hester

Outlook

LADY HESTER;

OR,

URSULA'S NARRATIVE.

by

CHARLOTTE M. YONGE

CHAPTER I.

SAULT ST. PIERRE.

I write this by desire of my brothers and sisters, that if any reports of our strange family history should come down to after generations the thing may be properly understood.

The old times at Trevorsham seem to me so remote, that I can hardly believe that we are the same who were so happy then. Nay, Jaquetta laughs, and declares that it is not possible to be happier than we have been since, and Fulk would have me remember that all was not always smooth even in those days.

Perhaps not—for him, at least, dear fellow, in those latter times; but when I think of the old home, the worst troubles that rise before me are those of the back-board and the stocks, French in the school-room, and Miss Simmonds' "Lady Ursula, think of your position!"

And as to Jaquetta, she was born under a more benignant star. Nobody could have put a back-board on her any more than on a kitten.

Our mother had died (oh! how happily for herself!) when Jaquetta was a baby, and Miss Simmonds most carefully ruled not only over us, but over Adela Brainerd, my father's ward, who was brought up with us because she had no other relation in the world.

Besides, my father wished her to marry one of my brothers. It would have done very well for either Torwood or Bertram, but unluckily, as it seemed, neither of them could take to the notion. She was a dear little thing, to be sure, and we were all very fond of her; but, as Bertram said, it would have been like marrying Jaquetta, and Torwood had other views, to which my father would not then listen.

Then Bertram's regiment was ordered to Canada, and that was the real cause of it all, though we did not know it till long after.

Bertram was starting out on a sporting expedition with a Canadian gentleman, when about ten miles from Montreal they halted at a farm with a good well-built house, named Sault St. Pierre, all looking prosperous and comfortable, and a young farmer, American in his ways—free-spoken, familiar, and blunt—but very kindly and friendly, was at work there with some French-Canadian labourers.

Bertram's friend knew him and often halted there on hunting expeditions, so they went into the house—very nicely furnished, a pretty parlour with muslin curtains, a piano, and everything pleasant; and Joel Lea called his wife, a handsome, fair young woman. Bertram says from the first she put him in mind of some one, and he was trying to make out who it could be. Then came the wife's mother, a neat little delicate, bent woman, with dark eyes, that looked, Bertram said, as if they had had some great fright and never recovered it. They called her Mrs. Dayman.

She was silent at first, and only helped her daughter and the maid to get the dinner, and an excellent dinner it was; but she kept on looking at Bertram, and she quite started when she heard him called Mr. Trevor. When they were just rising up, and going to take leave, she came up to him in a frightened agitated manner, as if she could not help it, and said—

"Sir, you are so like a gentleman I once knew. Was any relation of yours ever in Canada?"

"My father was in Canada," answered Bertram.

"Oh no," she said then, very much affected, "the Captain Trevor I knew was killed in the Lake Campaign in 1814. It must be a mistake, yet you put me in mind of him so strangely."

Then Bertram protested that she must mean my father, for that he had been a captain in the —th, and had been stationed at York (as Toronto was then called), but was badly wounded in repulsing the American attack on the Lakes in 1814.

"Not dead?" she asked, with her cheeks getting pale, and a sort of excitement about her, that made Bertram wonder, at the moment, if there could have been any old attachment between them, and he explained how my father was shipped off from England between life and death; and how, when he recovered, he found his uncle dying, and the title and property coming to him.

"And he married!" she said, with a bewildered look; and Bertram told her that he had married Lady Mary Lupton—as his uncle and father had wished—and how we four were their children. I can fancy how kindly and tenderly Bertram would speak when he saw that she was anxious and pained; and she took hold of his hand and held him, and when he said something of mentioning that he had seen her, she cried out with a sort of terror, "Oh no, no, Mr. Trevor, I beg you will not. Let him think me dead, as I thought him." And then she drew down Bertram's tall head to her, and fairly kissed his forehead, adding, "I could not help it, sir; an old woman's kiss will do you no harm!"

Then he went away. He never did tell us of the meeting till long after. He was not a great letter writer, and, besides, he thought my father might not wish to have the flirtations of his youth brought up against him. So we little knew!

But it seems that the daughter and son-in-law were just as much amazed as Bertram, and when he was gone, and the poor old lady sank into her chair and burst out crying, and as they came and asked who or what this was, she sobbed out, "Your brother Hester! Oh! so like him—my husband!" or something to that effect, as unawares. She wanted to take it back again, but of course Hester would not let her, and made her tell the whole.

It seems that her name was Faith Le Blanc; she was half English, half French-Canadian, and lived in a village in a very unsettled part, where Captain Trevor used to come to hunt, and where he made love to her, and ended by marrying her—with the knowledge of her family and his brother officers, but not of his family—just before he was ordered to the Lake frontier. The war had stirred up the Indians to acts of violence they had not committed for many years, and a tribe of them came down on the village, plundering, burning, killing, and torturing those whom they had known in friendly intercourse.

Faith Le Blanc had once given some milk to a papoose upon its mother's back, and perhaps for this reason she was spared, but everyone belonging to her was, she believed, destroyed, and she was carried away by the tribe, who wanted to make her one of themselves; and she knew that if she offended them, such horrors as she had seen practised on others would come on her.

However, they had gone to another resort of theirs, where there was a young hunter who often visited them, and was on friendly terms. When he found that there was a white woman living as a captive among them, he spared no effort to rescue her. Both he and she were often in exceeding danger; but he contrived her escape at last, and brought her through the woods to a place of safety, and there her child was born.

It was over the American frontier, and it was long before she could write to her husband. She never knew what became of her letter, but the hunter friend, Piers Dayman, showed her an American paper which mentioned Captain Trevor among the officers killed in their attack. Dayman was devoted to her, and insisted on marrying her, and bringing up her daughter as his own. I fancy she was a woman of gentle passive temper, and had been crushed and terrified by all she had gone through, so as to have little instinct left but that of clinging to the protector who had taken her up when she had lost everything else; and she married him. Nor did Hester guess till that very day that Piers Dayman was not her father!

There were other children, sons who have given themselves to hunting and trapping in the Hudson's Bay Company's territory; but Hester remained the only daughter, and they educated her well, sending her to a convent at Montreal, where she learnt a good many accomplishments. They were not Roman Catholics; but it was the only way of getting an education.

Dayman must have been a warm-hearted, tenderly affectionate person. Hester loved him very much. But he had lived a wild sportsman's life, and never was happy at rest. They changed home often; and at last he was snowed up and frozen to death, with one of his boys, on a bear hunting expedition.

Not very long after, Hester married this sturdy American, Joel Lea, who had bought some land on the Canadian side of the border, and her mother came home to live with them. They had been married four or five years, but none of their children had lived.

So it was when the discovery came upon poor old Mrs. Dayman (I do not know what else to call her), that Fulk Torwood Trevor, the husband of her youth, was not dead, but was Earl of Trevorsham; married, and the father of four children in England.

Poor old thing! She would have buried her secret to the last, as much in pity and love to him as in shame and grief for herself; and consideration, too, for the sons, for whom the discovery was only less bad than for us, as they had less to lose. Hester herself hardly fully understood what it all involved, and it only gradually grew on her.

That winter her mother fell ill, and Mr. Lea felt it right that the small property she had had for her life should be properly secured to her sons, according to the division their father had intended. So a lawyer was brought from Montreal and her will was made. Thus another person knew about it, and he was much struck, and explained to Hester that she was really a lady of rank, and probably the only child of her father who had any legal claim to his estates. Lea, with a good deal of the old American Republican temper, would not be stirred up. He despised lords and ladies, and would none of it; but the lawyer held that it would be doing wrong not to preserve the record. Hester had grown excited, and seconded him; and one day, when Lea was out, the lawyer brought a magistrate to take Mrs. Dayman's affidavit as to all her past history— marriage witnesses and all. She was a good deal overcome and agitated, and quite implored Hester never to use the knowledge against her father; but she must have been always a passive, docile being, and they made her tell all that was wanted, and sign her deposition, as she had signed her will, as Faith Trevor, commonly known as Faith Dayman.

She did not live many days after. It was on the 3rd of February, 1836, that she died; and in the course of the summer Hester had a son, who throve as none of her babies had done.

Then she lay and brooded over him and the rights she fancied he was deprived of, till she worked herself up to a strong and fixed purpose, and insisted upon making all known to her father. Now that her mother was gone she persuaded herself that he had been a cruel, faithless tyrant, who had wilfully deserted his young wife.

Joel Lea would not listen to her. Why should she wish to make his son a good-for-nothing English lord? That was his view. Nothing but misery, distress, and temptation could come of not letting things alone. He held to that, and there were no means forthcoming either of coming to England to present herself. The family were well to do, but had no ready money to lay out on a passage across the Atlantic. Nor would Hester wait. She had persuaded herself that a letter would be suppressed, even if she had known how to address it; but to claim her son's rights, and make an earl of him, had become her fixed idea, and she began laying aside every farthing in her power.

In this she was encouraged, not by the lawyer who had made the will—and who, considering that poor Faith's witnesses had been destroyed, and her certificate and her wedding ring taken from her by the Indians, thought that the marriage could not be substantiated—but by a clever young clerk, who had managed to find out the state of things; a man named Perrault, who used to come to the farm, always when Lea was out, and talk her into a further state of excitement about her child's expectations, and the injuries she was suffering. It was her one idea. She says she really believes she should have gone mad if the saving had not occupied her; and a very dreary life poor Joel must have had whilst she was scraping together the passage-money. He still steadily and sternly disapproved the whole, and when at two years' end she had put together enough to bring her and her boy home, and maintain them there for a few weeks, he still refused to go with her. The last thing he said was, "Remember, Hester, what was the price of all the kingdoms of the world! Thou wilt have it, then! Would that I could say, my blessing go with thee." And he took his child, and held him long in his arms, and never spoke one word over him but, "My poor boy!"

CHAPTER II.

TREVORSHAM

I suppose I had better tell what we had been doing all this time. Adela and I had come out, and had a season or two in London, and my father had enjoyed our pleasure in it, and paid a good deal of court to our pretty Adela, because there was no driving Torwood into anything warmer than easy brotherly companionship.

In fact, Torwood had never cared for anyone but little Emily Deerhurst. Once he had come to her rescue, when she was only nine or ten years old, and her schoolboy cousins were teasing her, and at every Twelfth-day party since she and he had come together as by right. There was something irresistible in her great soft plaintive brown eyes, though she was scarcely pretty otherwise, and we used to call her the White Doe of Rylstone. Torwood was six or seven years older, and no one supposed that he seriously cared for her, till she was sixteen. Then, when my father spoke point blank to him about Adela, he was driven into owning what he wished.

My father thought it utter absurdity. The connection was not pleasant to him; Mrs. Deerhurst was always looked on as a designing widow, who managed to marry off her daughters cleverly, and he could believe no good of Emily.

Now Adela always had more power with papa than any of us. She had a coaxing way, which his stately old-school courtesy never could resist. She used when we were children to beg for holidays, and get treats for us; and even now, many a request which we should never have dared to utter, she could, with her droll arch way, make him think the most sensible thing in the world.

What odd things people can do who have lived together like brothers and sisters! I can hardly help laughing when I think of Torwood coming disconsolately up from the library, and replying, in answer to our vigorous demands, that his lordship had some besotted notion past all reason.

Then we pressed him harder—Adela with indignation, and I with sympathy—till we forced out of him that he had been forbidden ever to think or speak again of Emily, and all his faith in her laughed to scorn, as delusions induced by Mrs. Deerhurst.

"I'm sure I hope you'll take Ormerod, Adela," I remember he ended; "then at least you would be out of the way."

For Sir John Ormerod's courtship was an evident fact to all the family, as, indeed, Adela was heiress enough to be a good deal troubled with suitors, though she had hitherto managed to make them all keep their distance.

Adela laughed at him for his kind wishes, but I could see she meant to plead for him. She had her chance, for Sir John Ormerod brought matters to a crisis at the next ball; and though she thought, as she said, "she had settled him," he followed it up with her guardian, and Adela was invited to a conference in the library.

It happened that as she ran upstairs, all in a glow, she came on Torwood at the landing. She couldn't help saying in her odd half-laughing, half-crying voice—

"It will come right, Torwood; I've made terms, I'm out of your way."

"Not Ormerod!" he exclaimed.

"Oh! no, no!" I can hear her dash of scorn now, for I was just behind my brother, but she went on out of breath—

"You may go on seeing her, provided you don't say a word—till—till she's been out two years."

"Adela! you queen of girls, how have you done it?" he began, but she thrust him aside and flew up into my arms; and when I had her in her own room it came out, I hardly know how, that she had so shown that she cared for no one she had ever seen except my father, that they found they *did* love each other; and—and—in short they were going to be married.

Really it seemed much less wonderful then than it does in thinking of it afterwards. My father was much handsomer than any young man I ever saw, with a hawk nose, a clear rosy skin, pure pink and white like a boy's, curly little rings of white hair, blue eyes clear and bright as the sky, a tall upright soldierly figure, and a magnificent stately bearing, courteous and grand to all, but sweetly tender to a very few, and to her above all. It always had been so ever since he had brought her home an orphan of six years old from her mother's death-bed at Nice. And he was youthful, could ride or hunt all day without so much fatigue as either of his sons, and was as fresh and eager in all his ways as a lad.

And she, our pretty darling! I don't think Torwood and I in the least felt the incongruity of her becoming our step-mother, only that papa was making her more entirely his own.

I am glad we did not mar the sunshine. It did not last long. She came home thoroughly unwell from their journey to Switzerland, and never got better. By the time the spring had come round again, she was lying in the vault at Trevorsham, and we were trying to keep poor little Alured alive and help my poor father to bear it.

He was stricken to the very heart, and never was the same man again. His age seemed to come upon him all at once; and whereas at sixty-five he had been like a man ten years younger, he suddenly became like one ten years older; and though he never was actually ill, he failed from month to month.

He could not bear the sight or sound of the poor baby. Poor Adela had scarcely lived to hear it was a boy, and all she had said about it was, "Ursula, you'll be his mother." And, oh! I have tried. If love would do it, I think he could not be more even to dear Adela!

What a frail little life it was! What nights and days we had with him; doctors saying that skill could not do it, but care might; and nurses knowing how to be more effective than I could be; yet while I durst not touch him I could not bear not to see him. And I do think I was the first person he began to know.

Meantime, there was a great difference in Torwood. He had been very much of a big boy hitherto. No one but myself could have guessed that he cared for much besides a lazy kind of enjoyment of all the best and nicest things in this world. He did what he was told, but in an uninterested sort of way, just as if politics and county business, and work at the estate, were just as much tasks thrust on him as Virgil and Homer had been; and put his spirit into sporting, &c.

But when he was allowed to think hopefully of Emily, it seemed to make a man of him, and he took up all that he had to do, as if it really concerned him, and was not only a burden laid on him by his father.

And, as my father became less able to exert himself, Torwood came forward more, and was something substantial to lean upon. Dear fellow! I am sure he did well earn the consent he gained at last, though not with much satisfaction, from papa.

Emily had grown into great sweetness and grace, and Mrs. Deerhurst had gone on very well. Of course, people were unkind enough to say, it was only because she had such prey in view as Lord Torwood; but, whatever withheld her, it is certain that Emily only had the most suitable and reasonable pleasures for a young lady, and was altogether as nice, and gentle, and sensible, as could be desired. There never was a bit of acting in her, she was only allowed to grow in what seemed natural to her. She was just one of the nice simple girls of that day, doing her quiet bit of solid reading, and her practice, and her neat little smooth pencil drawing from a print, as a kind of duty to her accomplishments every day; and filling books with neat up-and- down MS. copies of all the poetry that pleased her. Dainty in all her ways, timid, submissive, and as it seemed to me, colourless.

But Fulk taught her Wordsworth, who was his great passion then, and found her a perfect listener to all his Tory hopes, fears, and usages.

Papa could not help liking her when she came to stay with us, after they were engaged, at the end of two years. He allowed that, away from her mother and all her belongings, she would do very well; and she was so pretty and sweet in her respectful fear of him—I might almost say awe—that his graceful, chivalrous courtesy woke up again; and he was beginning absolutely to enjoy her, as she became a little more confident and understood him better.

How well I remember that last evening! I was happier than I had been for weeks about little Alured: the convulsions had quite gone off, the teeth that had caused them were through, and he had been laughing and playing on my lap quite brightly—cooing to his mother's miniature in my locket. He was such an intelligent little fellow for eighteen months! I came down so glad, and it was so pleasant to see Emily, in her white dress, leaning over my father while he had gone so happily into his old delight of showing his prints and engravings; and Torwood, standing by the fire, watching them with the look of a conqueror, and Jaquetta—like the absurd child she loved to be—teasing them with ridiculous questions about their housekeeping.

They were to have Spinney Lawn bought for them, just a mile away, and the business was in hand. Jacquey was enquiring whether there was a parlour for The Cid, Torwood's hunter, whom she declared was as dear to him as Emily herself. Indeed, Emily did go out every morning after breakfast to feed him with bread. I can see her now on Torwood's arm, with big Rollo and little Malta rolling over one another after them.

Then came an afternoon when we had all walked to Spinney Lawn, laid out the gardens together, and wandered about the empty rooms, planning for them. The birds were singing in the March sunshine, and the tomtits were calling "peter" in the trees, and Jaquetta went racing about after the dogs, like a thing of seven years old, instead of seventeen. And Torwood was cutting out a root of primroses, leaves and all, for Emily, when we saw a fly go along the lane, and wondered, with a sort of idle wonder. We supposed it must be visitors for the parsonage, and so we strolled home, looking for violets by the way, and Jaquetta getting shiny studs of celandine. Ah! I remember those glistening stars were all closed before we came back.

Well, it must come, so it is silly to linger! There stood the fly at the hall-door, and the butler met us, saying—

"There's a person with his lordship, my lord. She would not wait till you came in, though I told her he saw no one on business without you—"

Torwood hastened on before this, expecting to see some importunate person bothering my father with a petition. What he did see was my father leaning back in his chair, with a white, confounded, bewildered look, and a woman, with a child on her lap, opposite. Her back was to the door, and Torwood's first impression was that she was a well-dressed impostor threatening him; so he came quickly to my father's side, and said—

"What is it father? I'm here."

My poor father put out his hand feebly to him, and said—

"It is all true, Torwood. God forgive me; I did not know it!"

"Know what?" he asked anxiously. "What is it that distresses you, father? Let me speak to this person—"

Then she broke out—not loud, not coarsely, but very determinately—"No, sir; you would be very glad to suppress me, and my child, and my evidence, no doubt; but the Earl of Trevorsham has acknowledged the truth of my claim, and I will not leave this spot till he has acknowledged my mother as his only lawful wife, and my child, Trevor Lea, as his only lawful heir!"

Torwood thought her insane and only said quietly, as he offered my father his arm, "I will talk it over with you presently; Lord Trevorsham is not equal to discuss it now."

"I see what you mean!" she said quickly. "You would like to make me out crazy, but Lord Trevorsham knows better. Do not you, my father?" she said, with a strong emphasis, the more marked, because it was concentrated, not loud.

My poor father was shuddering all over with involuntary trembling; but he put Torwood's hand away from him, and looked up piteously, as if his heart was breaking (as it was); but he spoke steadily. "It is true. It is true, Torwood. I was married to poor Faith, when I was a young man, in Canada. They sent me proofs that all had perished when the Indians attacked the village; but—" and then he put his hands over his face. It must have been dreadful to see; but Hester Lea was too much bent on her rights to feel a moment's pity; and she spoke on in a hard tone, with her eyes fixed on my brother's face.

"But you failed to discover that she was rescued from the Indians; gave birth to me, your daughter, Hester; and only died two years ago."

"You hear! My boy, my poor boy, forgive me; don't leave me to her," was what my poor father had said—he who had been so strong.

My brother saw what it all meant now. "Never fear that, sir," he said; "I am your son still, any way, you know."

"You will do justice to me," she began, in her fierce tone; but my brother met it calmly with, "Certainly, we will do our best that justice should be done. You have brought proof?"

His quietness overawed her, and she pointed to the papers on the table. They were her mother's attested narrative, and the certificate of her burial.

My brother read aloud, "The 3rd of February, 1836," then he turned to my father and said, "You observe, father, the difference this may make, if true, is that of putting little Alured into the place I have held. My father's last marriage was on the 15th of April, 1836," he added to her. He says she quite glared at him with mortification, as if he had invented poor little Alured on purpose to baffle her; but my father breathed more freely.

"And is nothing—nothing to be done for my child, your own grandson?" exclaimed she, "after these years."

Torwood silenced her by one of his looks. "We only wish to do justice," he said. "If it be as you say, you will have a right to a great deal, and it will not be disputed; but you must be aware that a claim made in this manner requires investigation, and you can see that my father is not in a state for an exciting discussion."

"*Your* father!" she said, with a bitter tone of scorn; but he took it firmly, though the blood seemed to come boiling to his temples.

"Yes," he said, "my father! and if you are indeed his daughter, you should show some pity and filial duty, by not forcing the discussion on him while he can so little bear it."

That staggered her a little, but she said, "I do not wish to do him any harm, but I have my child's interests to think of. How do I know what advantage may be taken against him?"

Torwood saw my father lying back in the chair, trembling, and he dreaded a fit every moment.

"I give you my word," he said, "that no injustice shall be done you;" and as she looked keenly at him, as if she distrusted him, he said, "Yes, you may trust me. I was bred an English gentleman, whatever I was born, and I promise you never to come between you and your rights, when your identity as Lord Trevorsham's daughter is fully established. Meantime, do you not see that your presence is killing him? Tell me where you may be heard of?"

"I shall stay at the Shinglebay Hotel till I am secure of the justice I claim," she said. "Come, my boy, since your own grandfather will not so much as look at you."

Torwood walked her across the hall. He was a little touched by those last words, and felt that she might have looked for a daughter's reception, so he said in the hall—

"You must remember this is a very sudden shock to us all. When my father has grown accustomed to the idea, no doubt he will wish to see you again; but in his present state of health, he must be our first consideration. And unprepared as my sisters are, it would be impossible to ask you to stay in the house."

She was always a little subdued by my brother's manner; I think its courtesy and polish almost frightened her, high-spirited, resolute woman as she was.

"I understand," she said, with a stiff, cold tone. Jaquetta heard the echo of it, and wondered.

"But," he added, "when they understand all, and when my father is equal to it, you shall be sent for."

When he went back to the library he found my poor father unconscious. It was really only fainting then, and he came round without anyone being called, and he shrank from seeing anyone but Torwood, explaining to him most earnestly how, though he was too ill himself to go to the place, his brother-officer, General Poyntz, had done so for him, and had been persuaded that the whole settlement and all the inhabitants had been swept off. It was such a shock to him that it nearly killed him. Poor father! it was grievous to hear him wish it had quite done so!

We only knew that the woman had upset my father very much, and that Torwood could not leave him. Word was sent us to sit down to dinner without them, and Torwood sent for some gravy soup and some wine for him. He went on talking—sometimes about us, but more often about poor Faith, who seemed to have come back on him in all the beauty and charm of his first love. He seemed to be talking himself feverish, and after a time Torwood thought that silence would be better for him; so he got him to go to bed, and sent good old Blake, the butler, who had been his servant in the army, to sit in the dressing-room. Blake, it turned out, had known all about the old story, so he was a safe person. Not that safety mattered much. "Lady Hester Lea"—she called herself so now, as, indeed, she had every right—was making it known at Shinglebay.

So Torwood came out. I was very anxious, of course, and had been hovering about on the nursery stairs, where I had gone to see whether baby was quietly asleep, and I overtook him as he was going down-stairs.

"How is papa?" I asked.

I shall never forget the white look of the face he raised up to mine as he said, "Poor father! Ursula, I can only call the news terrible. Will you try to stand up against it bravely?"

And then he held out his arms and gathered me into them, and I believe I said, "I can bear anything when you do that!"

I thought it could only be something about Bertram, who had rather a way of getting into scrapes, and I said his name; but just as Fulk was setting me at ease on that score, Jaquetta, who was on the watch, too, opened the door of the green drawing-room, and we were obliged to go in. Then, hardly answering her and Emily, as they asked after papa, he stood straight up in the middle of the rug and told us, beginning with—"Ursula, did you know that our father had been married as a young man in Canada?"

No. We had never guessed it.

"He was," my brother went on, "This is his daughter."

"Our sister!" Jaquetta asked. "Where has she been all this time?"

But I saw there must be more to trouble him, and then it came. "I cannot tell. My father had every reason to believe that—she—his first wife—had been killed in a massacre by the Red Indians; but if what this person says is true, she only died two years ago. But it was in all good faith that he married our mother. He had taken all means to discover—"

Even then we did not perceive what this involved. I felt stunned and numbed chiefly from seeing the great shock it had been to my father and to him; but poor little Jaquetta and Emily were altogether puzzled; and Jaquetta said, "But is this sister of ours such a very disagreeable person, Torwood? Why didn't you bring her in and show her to us?"

Then he exclaimed, almost angrily at her simplicity, "Good heavens! girls, don't you see what it all means? If this is true, I am not Torwood. We are nothing—nobody—nameless."

He turned to the fire, put both elbows on the mantelshelf, and hid his face in his hands. Emily sprang up, and tried to draw down his arm; and she did, but he only used it to put her from him, hold her off at arm's length, and look at her—oh! with such a tender face of firm sorrow!

"Ah! Emily," he said; "you too! It has been all on false pretences! That will have to be all over now."

Then Emily's great brown eyes grew bigger with wonder and dismay.

"False pretences!" she cried, "what false pretences? Not that you cared for me, Torwood."

"Not that I cared for you," he said, with a suppressed tone that made his voice *so* deep! "Not that *I* cared, but that Lord Torwood did—Torwood is the baby upstairs."

"But it is you—you—you—Fulk!" said Emily, trying to creep and sidle up to him, white doe fashion. I believe nobody had ever called him by his Christian name before, and it made it sweeter to him, but still he did not give in.

"Ah! that's all very well," he said, and his voice was softer then, "but what would your mother say?"

"The same as I do," said Emily, undauntedly. "How should it change one's feelings one bit," and she almost cried at being held back.

He did let her nestle up to him then, but with a sad sort of smile. "My child, my darling," he said, "I ought not to allow this! It will only be the worse after!"

But just then a servant's step made them start back, and a message came and brought word that Mr. Blake would be glad if Lord Torwood would step up.

Yes, my poor father was wandering in his speech, and very feverish, mixing up Adela and Faith Le Blanc strangely together sometimes, and at others fancying he was lying ill with his wound, and sending messages to Faith.

15

We sent for the doctor, but he could not do anything really. It had been a death-blow, though the illness lasted a full week. He knew us generally, and liked to see us, but he always had the sense that something dreadful had happened to us; and he would stroke my hand or Jaquetta's, and pity us. He was haunted, too, by the sense that he ought to do something for us which he could not do. We thought he meant to make a will, securing us something, but he was never in a condition in which my brother would have felt justified in getting him to sign it. Indeed there was so little disease about him, and we thought he would get better, if only we could keep him free from distress and excitement; so we made his room as quiet as possible, and discouraged his talking or thinking.

Lady Hester came every day. My brother had sent for Mr. Eagles, our solicitor, to meet her the first time, and look at her papers.

He said he could not deny that it looked very bad for us. Of the original marriage there was no doubt; indeed, my father had told Torwood where to find the certificate of it, folded up in the secret drawer of his desk, with his commission in the army; and the register of Faith's burial was only too plain. The only chance there was for us was, that her identity could not be established; but Mr. Eagles did not think it would go off on this. The whole of her life seemed to be traceable; besides, there was something about Hester that forbade all suspicion of her being a conscious impostor. Whether she would be able to prove herself my father's daughter was another more doubtful point. That, however, made no difference, except as to her own rank and fortune. If the first wife were proved to have been alive till 1836, then little Alured was the only true heir to the title and estate, and, next after him, stood Hester Lea and her son.

People said she was like the family; I never could see it, and always thought the likeness due to their imagination. She took one by surprise. She was a tall, well-made woman, with a narrow waist, and a proud, peculiarly upright bearing, though quick, almost sharp in all her movements, and especially with her eyes. Those eyes, I confess, always startled me. They were clear, bright blue, well opened eyes—honest eyes one would have called them
—only they appeared to be always searching about, and darting at one when one least expected it. The red and white of the face too always had a clear hard look, like the eyes; the teeth projected a little, and were so very, very white, that they always seemed to me to flash like the eyes; and if ever she smiled, it was as much as to say, "I don't believe you." Her nose had an amount of hook, too, that always gave me the feeling of having a wild hawk in the room with me. Jaquetta used to call her a panther of the wilderness, but to my mind there was none of the purring cattish tenderness of the panther.

However, that might be only because she viewed us as her natural enemies, and was always on her guard against us, though I do not well know why; I am sure we only wanted to know the truth and do justice, and Fulk was so convinced that she would prove her case, and that there was no help for it, that at the end of hearing Mr. Eagles question her, he said, "Well, the matter must be tried in due time, but since we are brothers and sisters, let us be friendly," and he held out his hand to her. Mr. Eagles, who told me, said he could have beaten him for the imprudent admission, only he did look so generous and sweet and sad; and Lady Hester drew herself up doubtfully and proudly, as if she could hardly bear to own such a brother, but she did take his hand, coldly though, and saying, "Let me see my father."

He was obliged to tell her that this was impossible. I doubt whether she ever believed him—at least she used to gaze at him with her determined eyes, as if she meant to abash him out of falsehood, and she sharply questioned every one about Lord Trevorsham's state.

The determination to be friendly made my brother offer to take her to us. She consented, but not very readily, and I am afraid we were needlessly cold and dry; but we were taken by surprise when my brother brought her into the sitting-room. It was not very easy to welcome the woman who was going to turn us all out, and under such a stigma; and she—she could hardly be expected to look complacently at the interlopers who had her place, and the title she had a right to.

She put us through her hard catechism about my dear father's state, and said at last that she should like to see Lord Torwood.

Taken by surprise, we looked and signed towards him whom that name had always meant. He smiled a little and said, "Little Alured! But, remember, I am bound to concede nothing till judicial minds are convinced. The parties concerned cannot judge. Can you venture to have Baby down, Ursula?"

No, I did not venture. I thought it might have been averted; but I was only obliged to take her up to the nurseries. On the way up she asked which way my father's room lay. I answered, "Oh! across there;" I did not know if she might not make a dash at it.

I think she must have heard at Shinglebay how delicate poor little Alured was, and thence gathered hopes of the succession for her boy, for she asked her sharp questions about his health all the way up, and knew that he had had fits. I could not put her down as one generally can inquisitive people. I suppose it was because she was more sensible of the difference in our real positions than I have as yet felt.

Baby was asleep; and I think she was touched by the actual sight of him.

She said he was very like her boy; and though I supposed that a mere assertion at the time, it was quite true. Alured and Trevor Lea have always been remarkably alike. However, she cross-examined Nurse about his health even more minutely, and then took her leave; but she came again every day, walking after the first, as long as my dear father lived.

And she must have talked, for there came a kind of feeling over everyone, as well as ourselves, that something was hanging over us, of which the issue would be known when my father's illness took some turn.

Mr. Decies came every day to inquire, but I could not bear a strange eye, and Hester might have been looking on. I was steeling myself against him. Was I right?—oh! was I right? I have wondered and grieved! For I knew well enough what he had been thinking of for months before; only I did not want it to come to a point. How was I to leave little Alured to Jaquetta? or disturb my father by breaking up his home? I liked him on the whole, and had come the length of thinking that if I ever married at all, it would be— But that's all nonsense; and mine could not have been what other people's love was, or I should not have shrunk from the sight and look of him. If it had been only poverty that was coming, it would have been a different thing; but to be nameless impostors!

Mrs. Deerhurst had gone out on a round of visits, when Emily came to us, taking her younger daughter. They were not a very letter-writing family. It is odd how some people's pen is a real outlet of expression; while others seem to lack the nerve that might convey their thoughts to it, even when they live in more sympathy than Emily could well have had with her mother.

At least, so I understand, what afterwards we wondered at, that Emily never mentioned Hester; only saying, when, after some days she did write, that Lord Trevorsham was ill.

So Fulk had the one comfort of being with her when he was out of the sick room. I used to see them from the window walking up and down the terrace in the blue east wind haze of those March days, never that I could see speaking. I don't think my brother would have felt it honourable to tie one additional link between himself and her. He had not a doubt as to how her mother would act, but to be in her dear little affectionate presence was a better help than we could give him, even though nothing passed between them.

Jaquetta used to wonder at them, and then try to go on the same as usual; and would wander about the garden and park with her dogs, and bring us in little anecdotes, and do all the laughing over them herself. Poor child! she felt as if she were in a bad dream, and these were efforts to shake it off, and wake herself.

After all, nothing was ever so bad as those ten days! But, my brother always said he was thankful for the respite and time for thought which they gave him.

CHAPTER III.

THE PEERAGE CASE.

The end came suddenly at last, when we were thinking my dear father more tranquil. He passed away in sleep late one evening, just ten days after Hester's arrival. She had gone back to her lodgings, and we did not send to tell her till the morning; but by nine o'clock she was in the house.

We had crept down to breakfast, Jaquetta and I, feeling very dreary in the half-light, and as if desolation had suddenly come on us; and when we heard her fly drive up to the door, Jaquetta cried out almost angrily, "Torwood, how could you!" and we would have run away, but he said, "Stay, dear girls; it is better to have it over."

As she came in he rang the bell as if for family prayers, and she had only asked one or two questions, which he answered shortly, when all the servants came in, some crying sadly. Fulk read a very few prayers—as much as he had voice for, and then, as all stood up, he had to clear his voice, but he spoke firmly enough.

"It is right that you all should know that a grave doubt has arisen as to my position here. Lord Trevorsham had every reason to believe his first wife had perished by the hands of the Red Indians long before he married my mother. What he did was done in entire ignorance—no breath of blame must light on him. This lady alleges that she can produce proofs that she is his daughter, and that her mother only died in February, '36. If these proofs be considered satisfactory by a committee of the House of Lords, then she and Alured Torwood Trevor will be shown to be his only legitimate children. I shall place the matter in the right hands as soon as possible—that is" (for she was glaring at him), "as soon as the funeral is over. Until that decision is made I request that no one will call me by the title of him who is gone; but I shall remain here to take care of my little brother, whose guardian my father wished me to be; and for the present, at least, I shall make no change in the establishment."

I think everyone held their breath: there was a great stillness over all—a

19

sort of hush of awe—and then some of the maids began sobbing, and the butler tried to say something, but he quite broke down; and just then a troubled voice cried out—

"Torwood, Torwood, what is this?"

And there we saw Bertram in the midst of us, with the haggard look of a man who had travelled all night, and a dismayed air that I can never forget.

He had been quartered at Belfast, and we had written to him the day after my father's illness, to summon him home, but there were no telegraphs nor railways; and there had been some hindrance about his leave, so that it had taken all that length of time to bring him. Fulk had left all to be told on his arrival. He had come by the mail-coach, and walked up from the Trevorsham Arms, where he had been told of our father's death; and so had let himself in noiselessly, and was standing in the dining-room door, hearing all that Fulk said!

Poor fellow! Jaquetta flung herself on him, hiding her face against him, while the servants went, and before any one else could speak, Hester stood forth, and said, to our amazement—

"Captain Trevor! You know me. You can and must bear me witness, and do me justice—"

"You! I have seen you before—but—where? I beg your pardon," he said, bewildered.

"You remember Sault St. Pierre farm?" she said.

"Sault St. Pierre! What? You are Mrs. Lea! Good heavens! Where is your mother?"

"My mother is dead, sir. You were the first person who made known to her that her husband, my father, was not dead, but had taken—or pretended to take—an English woman for his wife."

"Wait!" thundered Fulk, "whatever my father did was ignorantly and honourably done!"

Bertram was as pale as death, and looked from one of us to the other, and at last, he gasped out—

"And that—was what she meant?"

"There, sir," said Hester, turning to Torwood, "You see your brother cannot deny it! You will not refuse justice to me, and my son."

I fancy she expected that the house was to be given up to her, and that we were only to remain there on her sufferance, perhaps till after the funeral.

20

My brother spoke, "Justice will no doubt be done; but the question does not lie between you and me, but between me and Alured. It is, as I said, a peerage question—and will be decided by the peers. Incidentally, that enquiry will prove what is your position and rank, as well as what may or may not be ours. Any further points depend upon my father's will, and that will be in the hands of Mr. Eagles. I think you can see that it would be impossible, as well as unfeeling, to take any steps until after the funeral."

Whatever Hester Lea was, she was a high-spirited being, standing there, a solitary woman, a stranger, with all of us four, and one whole household, as it must have seemed, against her. I was outraged and shocked at her defiance at the time, but when, some time after, I re-read King John, I saw that there was something of Constance in her.

"That may be," she answered, "but when my child's interests are at stake, I cannot haggle over conventionalities and proprieties. I am the Earl of Trevorsham's only legitimate daughter, and I claim my right to remain in his house, and to take charge of my infant brother."

A sign from Fulk stopped me, as I was going to scream at this.

"Remember," he said, "your identity has yet to be proved."

"Your brother there must needs witness. He has done so."

"What do you witness to, Bertram?" asked Fulk.

"I do not know; I cannot understand," said Bertram. "I saw this person in a farm in Lower Canada, and there was an old lady who seemed to have known my father, and was very much amazed to find he was not killed in 1814. I did not hear her name, nor know whose mother she was, nor anything about her, nor what this dreadful business means."

"At any rate," said Fulk to her, "your claim to remain in the house must depend on the legal proof of the fact. My father's first marriage is undoubted, but absolute legal certainty that you are the child of that marriage alone can entitle you to take rank as his daughter; and, therefore, I am not compelled to admit your claim to remain here, though if you will refrain from renewing this discussion till after the funeral, I will not ask you to leave the house."

"I do not recognize your right to ask or not to ask," she said, undauntedly.

"I am either Lord Trevorsham's rightful heir—and it is not yet shown that I am not—or else I am the guardian he appointed for his son. I know this to be so, and Mr. Eagles, who will soon be here, will show it to you in the will if you wish it. Therefore, until the decision is made, when, if it goes against me, the child will no doubt be made a ward in Chancery, I am the person responsible for him and his property."

"I have no doubt you will take advantage of me and of every quibble against me;" and there at last she began to break down; "but if there is justice in heaven or earth my child shall have it, though you and all were leagued against him."

And there she began to sob. And those brothers of mine, they actually grew compassionate; they ran after wine; they called us to bring salts, and help her. Emily shuddered, and put her hands behind her; but Jaquetta actually ran up to the woman, and coaxed her and comforted her, when I had rather have coaxed a tigress.

But I had to go to the table and pour out tea and give it to her with all the rest. I don't know how we got through that breakfast. But we did, and then I made the housekeeper put her into the very best rooms. Anything if she would only stay there out of the way.

When I came back, I found Fulk explaining why he had spoken at once, and he said he felt that she would have no scruples about taking the initiative, and that everyone would be having surmises.

Poor Bertram was even more cut up than we were. It came more suddenly, and he felt as if it was all his doing. He had no hope, and he took all ours away. There had been something in the old woman that impressed him as genuine, and he had no doubt that she had known and loved our father. Nay, no one could suspect Hester of not believing in her own story; the only question was whether the links of evidence could be substantiated.

The next thing that happened—I can't tell which day it was—was Mrs. Deerhurst's coming, professing to be dreadfully shocked and overcome by my father's death, to take away Emily. She must be so much in our way. I, who saw her first, answered only by begging to keep her—our great comfort and the one thing that cheered and upheld my brother.

Mrs. Deerhurst looked keenly at me; and I began to wonder what she knew, but just then came Fulk into the room, with his calm, set, determined face. I knew he would rather speak without me, so I went away, and only knew what he could bear to tell me afterwards.

Mrs. Deerhurst had been a great deal kinder than he expected. No doubt she would not break the thing off while there was a shred of hope that he was an earl; but he could not drive her to allow, in so many words, that it must depend upon that.

He had quite made up his mind that it was not right to enjoy Emily's presence and the comfort it gave him, unless he was secure of Mrs.

Deerhurst's permitting the engagement under his possible circumstances.

I believe he nattered himself she would, and let her deceive him with thinking so, instead of, as we all did, seeing that what she wanted was to secure the credit of being constant and disinterested in case he retained his position. So, although she took Emily home, she left him cheered and hopeful, admiring her, and believing that she so regarded her daughter's happiness that, if he had enough to support her, she would overlook the loss of rank and title. He went on half the evening talking about what a remarkable woman Mrs. Deerhurst was; and, at any rate, it cheered him up through those worst days.

Our Lupton uncles came, and were frightfully shocked and incredulous; at least, Uncle George was. Uncle Lupton himself remembered something of my father having told him of a former affair in America.

They would not let Jaquetta and me go to the funeral; and they were wise, for Hester thrust herself in—but it is of no use to think about that. Indeed, there is not much to tell about that time, and I need not go into the investigation. It was all taken out of our hands, as my brother had said. Perrault came over from Canada, and brought his witnesses, but not Joel Lea. He had nothing to prove, had conscientious scruples about appearing in an English court of justice, and still hoped it would all come to nothing.

We stayed on at the London house—the lawyers said we ought, and that possession was "nine-tenths," &c. Besides, we wanted advice for Baby, who had been worse of late.

The end of it was that it went against us. Faith's marriage, her identity, and Hester's, were proved beyond all doubt, and little Alured was served Earl of Trevorsham. Poor child, how ill he was just then! It was declared water on the brain! I could hardly think about anything else; but they all said it seemed like a mockery, and that he would not bear the title a week. And then Lady Hester would have been, not Countess of Trevorsham, but Viscountess Torwood, and at any rate she halved the personal property: all that had been meant for us.

For we already knew that there was nothing in the will that could do us any good. All depended on my mother's marriage settlements, and as the marriage was invalid they were so much waste paper.

My uncles, to whom my poor mother's fortune reverted, would not touch it, and gave every bit back to us; but it was only 10,000 pounds, and what was that among the four of us?

I was in a sort of maze all the time, thinking of very little beyond dear little Alured's struggle for life, and living upon his little faint smiles when he was a shade better.

Jaquetta has told me more of what passed than I heeded at the time.

Our brothers decided not to retain the Trevor name, to which we had no right; but they had both been christened Torwood; after an old family custom, and they thought it best to use this still as a surname.

Bertram felt the shame, as he would call it, the most; but Fulk held up his head more. He said where there was no sin there was no shame; and that to treat ourselves as under a blot of disgrace was insulting our parents, who had been mistaken, but not guilty.

Bertram was determined against returning to his regiment, and it would have been really too expensive. His plan was to keep together, and lay out our capital upon a piece of ground in New Zealand, which was beginning to be settled.

Jaquetta was always ready to be delighted. Dear child, her head was full of log huts and Robinson Crusoe life, and cows to milk herself; and I really think she would have liked to go ashore in the Swiss family's eight tubs!

The thorough change, after all the sorrow, seemed delicious to her! I heard her and Bertram laughing down below, and wondered if they got the length of settling what dogs they would take out!

And Fulk! He really had almost persuaded himself that Emily would go with us; or at the very worst, would wait till he had achieved prosperity and could come home and fetch her.

Mrs. Deerhurst had declared that waiting for the decision was so bad for her nerves, that she must take her to Paris; and actually our dear old stupid fellow had not perceived what that meant, for the woman had let him part tenderly with Emily in London, with promises of writing, &c., the instant the case was decided. It passed his powers to suppose she could expose her daughter's heart to such a wreck. So he held up, cheerful and hopeful, thinking what a treasure of constancy he had! And when they had built their castle in New Zealand, they sent up Jaquey to call me to share it with them. Baby was asleep, and I went down; but when I heard the plan—it was cross to be so unsympathizing, but I did feel hurt and angry at their forgetting him; and I said, "I shall never leave Alured."

"Ursula! you could not stay by yourself," said Jaquey. And Bertram, who had hardly ever seen him, and could not care for him said it was nonsense, and even if there were a chance of the child living, I could not be left behind.

I was wrought up, and broke out that he would and should live, and that I would come as a stranger, a nursery governess, and watch over him, and never abandon him to Hester.

"Never fear, Ursula," said Fulk, "if he lives, he will be in safe hands."

"Safe hands! What are safe hands for a child like that! Hester's, who only wishes him out of her way?"

"For shame!" the others said, and I answered that, of course, I did not think Hester meant ill by him, but that, where the doctors had said only love and care could save him—no care was safe where he was not loved; and I cried very, very bitterly, more than I had done even for my father, or for anything else before; and I fell into a storm of passion, at the cruelty of leaving the poor little thing, whom his dying mother had trusted to me, and declared I would never, never do it.

I was right in the main, it seems to me, but unjust and naughty in the way I did it; and when Fulk, with some hesitation, began to talk of my not being asked to go just yet—not while the child lived—I turned round in a really violent, naughty fit, with—"You too, Fulk, I thought you loved your little brother better than that? You only want to be rid of him, and leave him to Hester, and he will die in her hands."

Fulk began to say that the Court of Chancery never gave the custody to the next heir. But I rushed away again to the nursery, and sat there, devising plans of disguising myself in a close cap and blue spectacles, and coming to offer myself as Lord Trevorsham's governess.

The child had no relations whatever on his mother's side, and though, if he had been healthy, nurses and tutors might have taken care of this baby lordship, even that would have been sad enough; and for the feeble little creature, whose life hung on a thread, how was it to be thought of? I fully made up my mind to stay, even if they all went. I told Jaquetta, so—in my vehemence dashed all her bright anticipation, and sent her again in tears to bed. I wish unhappiness would not make one so naughty!

The next day poor Fulk was struck down. A letter came from Mrs. Deerhurst to break off the engagement, and a great parcel containing all the things he had given Emily. She must have packed them up before leaving England, while she was still flattering him. Not a word nor a line was there from Emily herself!—only a supplication from the mother that he would not rend her child's heart by persisting—just as if she had not encouraged him to go on all this time!

Nothing would serve him but that he must dash over to Paris, to see her and Emily.

Railroads were not, and it was a ten days' affair at the shortest; and, with all our prospects doubtful and Alured still so ill, it was very trying. How Bertram did rave at the folly and futility of the expedition! but one comfort was, that Alured was a ward of Chancery, and, in the vast kindness and commiseration everyone bestowed upon us, no one tried to hurry us or turn us out.

Hester used to come continually to inquire after her brother, and there was something in her way that always made me shudder when she asked after him. I knew she could not wish for his life, and gloated over all the reports she could collect of his weakness. I felt more and more horror of her; God forgive me for not having tried not to hate her. I sometimes doubt whether my dread and distrust were not visible, and may not have put it into her head.

And then came Mr. Decies, again and again. He was faithful—I see it now. He cared not if I had neither name nor fortune; he held fast to his proposals. And I? Oh, I was absorbed—I was universally defiant—I did not do him justice in the bitterness I did not realise. I thought he was constant only out of honour and pity, and I did not choose to open my heart to understand his pleadings or accept them as earnest—I was harsh. Oh, how little one knows what one is doing! Too proud to be grateful—that was actually my case. I was enamoured of the blue-spectacle plan; I had romances of watching Alured day and night, and pouring away dangerous draughts. The very fancy, I see now, was playing with edged tools; I feel as if my imagination had put the possibility into the very air.

Once indeed—when Jaquetta had been telling me she did not understand my unkindness; and observed that, even for Alured's sake, she could not see why I did not accept—I did begin to regard him as a possible protector for the boy. But no; the blue spectacles would be the more assiduous guardian, said my foolish fancy.

Before I had thought it over into sense or reason, Fulk came back from Paris. He had not been really crushed till now. He was white, and silent, and resolute, and very gentle; all excitement of manner gone. He did not say one word, but we knew it was all over with him, and that he could not have had one scrap of comfort or hope.

Nor had he, though even to me he told nothing, till we were together in the dark one evening, much later. He did insist upon seeing Emily; but her mother would not leave her, or take her eyes off her, and the timid thing did nothing but sob and cry, in utter helplessness and shame, and never even gave him a look.

It was not the being neglected and cast off that he felt as such a wrong, to both himself and Emily, but the being drawn on with false hopes and promises to expect that she was to belong to him, after all; and he was cruelly disappointed that Emily had not energy to cling to him—he had made so sure of her.

Bertram and Jaquetta had expected all along that he would be the more eager to be off to the Antipodes when everything was swept away from him here, and he did sit after dinner talking it over in a business-like way, while Bertram gave him all the information he had been collecting in his absence.

I would not listen. I was determined against going away from my charge; I had rather have been his housemaid than have left him to Hester, and I must have looked like a stone as I got up, and left them to their talk while I went back to the boy.

I heard Bertram say while I was lighting my candle, "Poor Ursula! she will not see it. Hart told me to-day that the child is dying—would hardly get through the night."

Now I had been thinking all the afternoon that he was better, and I had gone down to dinner cheered. I turned into the doorway, and told Fulk to come and see.

He did come. There was Alured, lying, as he had lain all day, upon his nurse's knees, with her arm under his head. He had not moaned for a long time, and I had left him in a more comfortable sleep. He opened his eyes as we came in, held out his hands more strongly than we thought he could have done, quite smiled—such an intelligent smile—and said, "Tor—Tor—," which was what he had always called his brother, making his gesture to go to him.

The tears came into Fulk's eyes, though he smiled back and spoke in his sweet, strong voice, and held out his arms, while we told him he had better sit down. Poor nurse! she must have been glad enough—she had held him all that live-long day! And he was quite eager to go to his brother, and smiled up and cooed out, "Tor—Tor," again, as he felt himself on the strong arm.

Fulk bade nurse go and lie down, and he would hold him. And so he did. I fed the child, as I had done at intervals all day; and he sometimes slept, sometimes woke and murmured or cooed a little, and Fulk scarcely spoke or stirred, hour after hour. He had been travelling day and night, but, strange to say, that enforced calm—that tender stillness and watching, was better for him than rest. He would only have tossed about awake, if he had gone to bed after a discussion with Bertram.

But in the morning Dr. Hart came, quite surprised to find the child alive;

27

and when he looked at him and felt his pulse, he said, "You have saved him for this time, at least."

(Everybody was lavish of pronouns, and chary of proper names. Nobody knew what to call anybody.)

His little lordship was able to be laid in his cot, and Fulk, almost blind now with sheer sleep, stumbled off to his room, threw himself on his bed, and slept for seven hours in his clothes without so much as moving. He confessed that he had never had such unbroken, dreamless sleep since he had first seen Hester Lea's face.

That little murmur of "Tor—Tor" had settled all our fates. I don't think he had realised before how love was the one thing that the child's life hung upon, and that the boy himself must have that love and trust. Then, too, when he had waked and dressed and come down, the first person he met was Hester, with her hard, glittering eyes, trying to condole, and not able to hide how the exulting look went out of her face on hearing that the Earl (as she chose to term him) was better.

She supposed some arrangement would soon be made, and Fulk said he should see the lawyers at once about it, and arrange for the personal guardianship of Lord Trevorsham.

"Of course I am the only proper person while he lives, poor child," she said.

I broke in with, "The next heir is never allowed the custody."

I wish I had not. She hastily and proudly said "What do you mean?" and Fulk quickly added that "the Lord Chancellor would decide."

The next day he went out, and on returning came up to me in the nursery, and called me into the study.

"Ursula," he said, "I find that, considering the circumstances, there will be no objection made to our retaining the personal charge of our little brother. Everyone is very kind. Ours is not a common case of illegitimacy, and my father's well-known express wishes will be allowed to prevail."

"And your character," I could not help saying; and he owned that it did go for something, that he was known to everybody, and had some standing of his own, apart from the rank he had lost.

Then he went on to say that this would of course put an end to the emigration plan, so far as he was concerned. No doubt in the restless desire of change coming after such a fall and disappointment it was a great sacrifice; but as he said, "There did not seem anything left for him in life but just to try to do what seemed most like one's duty." And then he said it did not seem a worthy thing to do nothing, but just exist on a confined income, and the only thing he did know anything about, and was not too old to learn, was farming, and managing an estate.

Trevorsham would want an agent, for old Hall was so old, that my brother had really done all his work for a year or two past; and he had felt his way enough to know he could get appointed to the agency, if he chose. The house was to be let, but there was a farm to be had about two miles off, with a good house, and he thought of taking it, and stocking it, and turning regular farmer on his own account; while looking after the property, and bringing Alured up among his own people and interests.

Bertram did not like this at all. "Among all our old friends and acquaintance? Impossible! unbearable!" he said.

But Fulk's answer, was—"Better so! If we went to a strange place, and tried to conceal it, it would always be oozing out, and be supposed disgraceful. If my sisters can bear it, I had rather confront it straightforwardly —"

"And be *pitied*"—said Bertram, with *such* a contemptuous tone.

Nobody, however, thought it would be advisable for him to give up the New Zealand plan, nor did he ever mean it for a moment; indeed, he declared that he should go and prepare for us; for that we should very soon get tired of Skimping's Farm, and come out to him; meaning, of course, that our dear charge would be over.

He even wanted Jaquetta to come with him at once, and the log huts and fern trees danced before her eyes as the blue spectacles had done before mine; but she did not like to leave me, and Fulk would not encourage it, for we both thought her much too young and too tenderly brought up to be sent out to a wild settler's life alone with Bertram, and without a friend near.

To be farmers' sisters where we had been the Earl's daughters—well, I had much rather then that it had been somewhere else; but I saw it was best for Baby and still more so for Fulk, and clear little Jaquey held fast to me and to him, and so it was settled!

Our friends and relatives had much rather we had all emigrated. They did not know what to do with us, and would have been glad to have had us all out of sight for ever, "damaged goods shipped off to the colonies." We felt this and it heartened us up to stay out of the spirit of opposition.

Old Aunt Amelia, who fussed and cried over us, and our two uncles, who gave us good advice by the yard! Alas! I fear we were equally ungrateful to them, both cold and impatient. No, we did not bear it really well, though they said we did. We had plenty of pride and self-respect, and that carried us on; but there was no submission, no notion of taking it religiously. I don't mean that we did not go to church, and in the main try to do right. Any one more upright than my brother it would have been hard to find; but as to any notion that religious feeling could help us, and that our reverse might be blessed to us, that would have seemed a very strange language indeed!

And so we were hard, we would bear no sympathy but from one another, and even among ourselves we never gave way.

People admired us, I fancy, but were alienated and disappointed, and we were quite willing *then* to have it so.

CHAPTER IV.

SKIMPING'S FARM.

Skimping's Farm was the unlucky name of the place, and Fulk would allow of no modification—his resolution was to accept it all entirely. Now I love no spot on earth so well. It was very different then.

The farm-house lay on the slope of the hill, in the parish of Trevorsham, but with the park lying between it and the main village. The ground sloped sharply down to the little river, which, about two miles lower down, blends with the Avon, being, in fact, a creek out of Shinglebay. Beneath the house the stream is clear and rocky, but then comes a flat of salt marsh, excellent for cattle; and then, again, the river becomes tidal, and reaches at high water to the steep banks, sometimes covered with wood, sometimes with pasture or corn.

Then under the little promontory comes the hamlet of fisherfolk at Quay Trevor; and then the coast sweeps away to Shinglebay town, as anyone may see by the map.

Ours is an old farm, and had an orchard of old apple-trees sloping down to the river—as also did the home field, only divided by a low stone wall from the little strip of flower-garden before the house, which in those days had nothing in it but two tamarisks, a tea-tree, and a rose with lovely buds and flowers that always had green hearts.

There was a good-sized kitchen-garden behind, and the farm-yard was at the side by the back door. The house is old and therefore was handsome outside, even then, but the chief of the lower story was comprised in one big room, a "keeping-room," as it was called, with an open chimney, screened by a settle, and with a long polished table, with a bench on either side. Into this room the front porch—a deep one, with seats—opened. At one end was a charming little sitting-room, parted off; at the other, the real kitchen for cooking, and the dairy and all the rest of the farm offices.

Up-stairs—the stairs are dark oak, and come down at one end of the big kitchen—there is one beautiful large room, made the larger by a grand oriel window under the gable, one opening out of it, and four more over the offices; then a step-ladder and a great cheese-room, and a perfect wilderness of odd nooks up in the roof.

As to furniture, Fulk had bought that with the stock and everything else belonging to the farm for a round sum; and the Chancery people told us that we might take anything for ourselves from home that had been bought by ourselves, had belonged to our mother, or been given to us individually.

So the furniture of Fulk's rooms in London—most of which he had had at Oxford—my own piano, our books, and various little worktables, chairs, pictures, and knicknacks appertained to us; also, we brought what belonged to the little one's nursery, and put him in the large room. His grand nurse—Earl though he was—could not stand the change; but old Blake, who was retiring into a public house, as he could do nothing else for us, suggested his youngest sister, who became the comfort of my life, for she was the widow of a small farmer, and could give me plenty of sound counsel as to how much pork to provide for the labourers, and how much small beer would keep them in good heart, and not make them too merry. And she had too much good sense to get into rivalry with Susan Sisson, the hind's wife, who lived in a kind of lean-to cottage opening into the farm-yard, and was the chief (real) manager of the dairy and poultry—though such was not Jaquetta's view of the case by any manner of means.

What a help it was to have one creature who did enjoy it all from the very first!

The parting with Bertram was sore, and one's heart will ache after him still at times, though he is prosperous and happy with his wife and fine family at the new Trevorsham. Fulk went through it all in a grave set way, as if he knew he never should be happy again, and accepted everything in silence, as a matter of course, not wanting to sadden us, but often grieving me more by his steady silence than if he had complained.

One thing he was resolved on, that he would be a farmer out and out—not a gentleman farmer, as he said; but though he only wore broadcloth in the evening and on Sundays, I can't say he ever succeeded in not looking more of the gentleman.

We fitted up the little parlour with our prettiest things, and it was our morning room, and we put a screen across the big keeping-room, which made it snug for a family gathering place. But those were the days when everyone was abusing the farmers for not living with their labourers in the house, and Fulk was determined to try it, at least the first year, either for the sake of consistency, or because he was resolved to keep our expenses as low as possible. "Failure would be ruin," he impressed on us, and he thought we ought to live on the profits of the farm, except what was directly spent on the boy, and to save the income of the agency. (Taking one year with another, we did so.)

So he gave up his own dear old Cid, and only used the same horses that had sufficed for our predecessor—a most real loss and deprivation—and he chose to take meals at the long table in the keeping-room with the farm servants. He said we girls might dine in our little parlour apart, but there was no bearing that, and the whole household dined and supped together. Breakfast was at such uncertain times that we left that for the back kitchen, and had our own little round table by the fire, or in the parlour, at half-past seven; and so we took care to have a good cup of coffee for Fulk when he came in about five or six; but the half-past twelve dinner and eight o'clock supper were at the long table, our three selves and Baby at the top—Baby between me and Mrs. Rowe ("Ally's Rowe," as he called her), then George and Susan Sisson opposite each other, the under nurse, the two maids, the hind, and the three lads.

I believe it was a very awful penance to them at first. We used to hear them splashing away at the pump and puffing like porpoises; and they came in with shining faces and lank hair in wet rats' tails, the foremost of which they pulled on all occasions of sitting down, getting up, or being offered food.

But they always behaved very well, and the habit of the animal at feeding-time is so silent that I believe the restraint was compensated by the honour; and it did civilise them, thanks, perhaps, to Susan's lectures on manners, which we sometimes overheard.

Fulk made spasmodic attempts to talk to Sisson; but the chief conversation was Jaquetta's. She went on merrily all dinner-time, asking about ten thousand things, and hazarding opinions that elicited amusement in spite of ourselves: as when she asked, what sheep did with their other two legs, or suggested growing canary seed, as sure to be a profitable crop. Indeed, I think she had a little speculation in it on her own account in the kitchen garden— only the sparrows were too many for her—and what they left would not ripen.

But the child was always full of some new and rare device, rattling on anyhow, not for want of sense, but just to force a smile out of Fulk and keep us all alive, as she called it. She knew every bird and beast on the farm, fed the chickens, collected the eggs, nursed tender chicks or orphan lambs and weaning calves, and was in and out with the dogs all day, really as happy as ten queens, with the freedom and homely usefulness of the life—tripping daintily about in the tall pattens of farm life in those days, and making fresh enjoyment and fun of everything.

I used to be half vexed to see her grieve so little over all we had lost; but

Fulk said, "I suppose it is very hard to break down a creature at that age."

And even I was cheered by the wonderful start of health Alured took from the time Mrs. Rowe had him. He grew fat and rosy, and learnt to walk; and Dr. Hart was quite astonished at his progress, and said he was nearly safe from any more attacks of that fearful water on the brain till he was six or seven years old, and that, till that time, we must let him be as much as possible in the open air, and with the animals, and not stimulate his brain— neither teach, nor excite, nor contradict him, nor let him cry. The farm life was evidently the very thing he wanted.

What a reprieve it was, even though it should be only a reprieve!

He was already three years old, and was very clever and observant.

We were glad that he was too young to take heed of the change, or to see what was implied by his change from "baby," to "my lord," and we always called him by his Christian name. Mrs. Rowe felt far too much for us to gossip to him, and he was always with her or with me, though I do believe he liked Ben—the great, rough, hind—better than anyone else; would lead Mrs. Rowe long dances after him, to see him milk the cows, and would hold forth to him at dinner, in a way as diverting to us as it was embarrassing to poor Ben, who used to blurt out at intervals, "Yoi, my lord," and "Noa, my lord," while the two maids tried to swallow their tittering. The farmers at market used to call Fulk, "my lord," by mistake, and then colour up to their eyes through their red faces.

I believe, indeed, it was their name for him among themselves, and that they watched him with a certain contemptuous compassion, in the full belief that he would ruin himself.

And he declares he should if he had lived a bit more luxuriously, or if he had not had the agency salary to help him through the years of buying experience and the bad season with which he began.

Nor was it till he had for some years introduced that capital breed which thrives so well in the salt marshes, and twice following showed up the prize ox at the county show, that they began to believe in "Farmer Torwood," or think his "advanced opinions" in agriculture anything but a gentleman's whimsies.

As to friends and acquaintance, I am afraid we showed a great deal of pride and stiffness. They were kinder than we deserved, but we thought it prying and patronage, and would not accept what we could not return.

It is not fair to say we. It was only myself—Jaquetta never saw anything but kindness, and took it pleasantly, and Fulk was too busy and too unhappy to be concerned about our visiting matters. If I saw anyone coming to call I hid myself in the orchard, or if I was taken by surprise I was stiffness itself; and then I wrote a set of cards (Miss Torwood and Miss Jaquetta Torwood), and drove round in the queer old-fashioned gig to leave them, and there was an end of it; for I would accept no invitations, though Jaquetta looked at me wistfully. And thus I daunted all but old Miss Prior. Poor old thing! All her pleasures had oozed down from our house in old times to her; and her gratitude was indomitable, and stood all imaginable rebuffs that courtesy permitted me. I believe she only pitied and loved me the more, and persevered in the dreadful kindness that has no tact.

It did not strike me that pleasure might be good for Jaquetta, or that Fulk's stern silent sorrow might have been lightened by variety. Used as he had been to political life and London society, it was no small change to have merely the market for interest, the farm for occupation, and no society but ourselves; no newspaper but the County Chronicle once a week; no new books, for Mudie did not exist then, even if we could have afforded it. We had dropped out of the guinea country book club, and Knight's "Penny Magazine" was our only fresh literature. However, Jaquetta never was much of a reader, and was full of business—queen of the poultry, and running after the weakly ones half the day, supplementing George Sisson's very inadequate gardening—aye, and his wife's equally rough cooking. She found a receipt book, and turned out excellent dishes. She could not bear, she said, to see Fulk try to eat grease, and with an effort at concealment, assisted by the dogs, fall back upon bread and cheese.

Luckily plain work in the school-room had not gone out in our day, and I could make and mend respectably, but I had to keep a volume of Shakespeare, Scott, or Wordsworth open before me, and learn it by heart, to keep away thoughts, which might have been good for me; but no—they were working on their own bitterness.

Sunday was the hardest day of all to Fulk, for this was the only one on which he could not be busy enough to tire himself out. We were a mile from church, and when we got to the worm-eaten farm pew there was a smell, as Jaquey said, as if generations of farmers had been eating cheese there, and generations of mice eating after them; and she always longed to shut up a cat there.

The old curate was very old, and nothing seemed alive but the fiddles in the gallery—indeed, after the "Penny Magazine" had made us acquainted with the Nibelung, Jaquey took to calling Sisson, Folker the mighty fiddler, so determined were his strains.

After the great house was shut up, one service was dropped, and so the latter part of the day was spent in a visit to all the livestock, Fulk laden with Alured, and Jaquetta with tit bits for each and all.

She and Alured really enjoyed it, and we tried to think we did! And then Fulk used to stride off on a long solitary walk, or else sit in the porch with his arms across, in a dumb heavy silence, till he saw us looking at him; and then he would shake himself, and go and find Sisson, and discuss every field and beast with him.

At least we thought we should have been at peace here; but one afternoon, when Jaquetta had gone across to the village to see some purchase at the shop, she came back flushed and breathless, and said as she sat down by me, "Oh! Ursie, Ursie, I met Miss Prior; and *she* has bought Spinney Lawn."

She was Hester; it had never meant anyone else amongst us when it was said in that voice. Fulk, when we told him, had, it appeared, known it for some days past. All he said was, "Well! she has every right."

And when I exclaimed, "Just like a harpy, come to watch our poor child!" he said, "Nonsense."

But I knew I was right, and sat brooding—till presently he said, "Put that out of your head, Ursula, or you will not be able to behave properly to her."

"I don't see any good in behaving properly to her," said Jaquetta. "What business has she to come here?"

"I do not choose to regale the neighbourhood with our family jars"—said Fulk, quietly.

And then—such a ridiculous child as Jaquetta was—she burst out laughing, and cried, "What a feast they would be! Preserved crabs, I suppose;" and she brought a tiny curl into the corner of his mouth.

My pride was up, and I remember I answered, "You are right, Fulk. No one shall say we are jealous, or shrink from the sight of her!"

"When Smith told me that he had no idea who was the bidder, or he would not have suffered it," said Fulk, "I told him I could have no possible objection!"

And so we endured it in our pride and our dignity.

Lady Hester Lea was the heroine of the neighbourhood. The romance of the disowned daughter was charming; and I was far too disagreeable to excite any counterbalancing pity. She was handsome, and everybody raved about her likeness to poor papa and the family portraits; and her Montreal convent had given her manners quite distinct from English vulgarity; or, maybe, her blood told on her bearing, for she was immensely admired for her demeanour, quite as much as for her beauty.

Old Miss Prior—whom no coldness on my part could check in her assiduous kindness, and nothing would hinder from affectionately telling us whatever we did not want to hear—kept us constantly informed of the new comer's triumphs. Especially she would dwell upon the sensation that Lady Hester produced, and all that the gentlemen said of her. Her name stood as lady patroness to all the balls and fancy fairs, and archery, that Shinglebay produced; and there was no going to shop there without her barouche coming clattering down the street with the two prancing greys, and poor little Trevor inside, with a looped-up hat and ostrich feather exactly like Alured's; for by some intention she always dressed him in the exact likeness of his little uncle's. I used to think Miss Prior told her, and sedulously prevented her ever seeing his lordship out of his brown holland pinafores, but the same rule still held good.

What tender enquiries poor Miss Prior used to make after "the dear little lord," as she called him. My asseverations of his health and intelligence generally eliciting that it was current among Lady Hester's friends that he could neither stand nor speak, and was so imbecile that it was a mercy that he could not live to be eight years old.

Of course that was what Hester was waiting for. And no small pleasure was it when Alured would come pattering in with a shout of "Ursa, Ursa," and as soon as he saw a lady, would stop, and pull off his hat from his chestnut curls like the little gentleman he always was.

Spinney Lawn was bought before Joel Lea came to England. If he had seen where it was I doubt whether he would have consented to the purchase; but Perrault managed it all, and then, with what he had made out of the case, bought himself a share in Meakin's office at Shinglebay, and constituted himself Lady Hester's legal adviser.

Mr. Lea, after vainly trying to get his wife to return to Sault St. Pierre, thought it wrong to be apart from her and his son, and came to England.

Fulk went at once to call on him, expecting to be disgusted with Yankeeisms; but came home, saying he had found a more unlucky man than himself!

Fancy a great, big, plain, hard-working back-woodsman, bred only to the axe and rifle, with illimitable forests to range in, happy in toil and homely plenty, and a little king to himself, set down in an English villa, with a trim garden and paddock, and servants everywhere to deprive him of the very semblance to occupation!

Poor man! he had not even the alleviation of being proud of it, and trying to live up to it. Puritan to the bone of his broad back, he thought everything as wicked as it was wearisome and foolish; and lived like Faithful in "Vanity Fair," solely enduring it for the sake of his wife and son. I suppose he could not have carried her off, or altered her course without the strong hand; for she was a determined woman, all the more resolute because she acted for her child.

He was a staunch Dissenter, and would not go to church with Lady Hester, who did so as a needful part of the belonging of her station, or, perhaps, to watch over us, but trudged two miles every Sunday to the meeting-house at Shinglebay, where he was a great light, and spent all that she allowed him on the minister and the Sunday school.

As to society, he abhorred it on principle, and kept out of the way when his wife gave her parties. If she had an old affection for him in the depths of her heart, it was swallowed up in vexation and provocation; and no wonder, for the verdict of society, as Miss Prior reported it, was—"How sad that such a woman as Lady Hester should have been thrown away on a mere common man—not a bit better than a labourer."

I detested him like all the rest; but Fulk declared he was sublime in passive endurance, and used to make opportunities of consulting him about cattle or farming, just to interest him.

Fulk and the dissenting minister were the only friends the poor man had, and the latter Hester would not let into her house. As to Perrault, he loathed and shrank from him as the real destroyer of all his peace, and still the most dangerous influence about his wife. He never said so, but we felt it.

I think the poor man's happiest hours were spent here; and, now and then in a press of work, or to show how a thing ought to be done, he put his own hand to axe, lever, or hay-fork, and toiled with that cruelly-wasted alert strength.

Fulk always says there never was anyone who taught him so much as Joel Lea, and he means deeper things than farming.

Sometimes Mr. Lea brought his little boy. I was vexed at first; but Alured, who had hardly spoken to a child before, was in ecstasies, as if a new existence had come upon him; and Trevor Lea was really a very nice little boy. He was only half a year the elder; and they were so much alike that strangers did not know them apart, dressed alike, as they were; or they were taken for twins, and it made people laugh to find they were uncle and nephew.

And I must allow the nephew was the best behaved, though it made me savage to hear Fulk say so. But our Ally's was not real naughtiness—only the consequence of our not being able to keep up discipline, while we lived in dread of that seventh year that might rob us of our darling—always sweet and loving.

CHAPTER V.

SPINNEY LAWN.

A change or two began to creep into our life. One afternoon, as Jaquetta, in her pretty pink gingham and white apron, with her black hair in the Grecian coil we used to wear when our heads were allowed to be of their own proper size, was gathering crimson apples from the quarrendon tree close to the river, a voice came over the water—

"Oh, my good girl, if you would but stand so a minute, and allow me to sketch you!"

Jaquetta started round and laughed. No doubt she was looking like an Arcadian; but I—as from under the trees I saw two gentlemen on the other side of the little stream, and jumped up to come to her defence—I must have looked more like a displeased if not draggle-tailed duchess, for there was an immediate disconcerted begging of our pardons, and a hasty departure.

Jaquetta made a very funny account of my spring forward in awful dignity, so horribly affronted at her being called a good girl! and she made Fulk laugh heartily. The gloom did seem to be lightening on him now.

Walking tourists, we supposed, though one we thought was a clergyman; and on Sunday we saw him in the desk and the draughtsman in the parsonage pew; and we discovered that these were the proposed new curate, Mr. Cradock, and his younger brother. Our rector was a canon who had bad health and never came near us, and the poor old curate was past work, and, indeed, died a week or two after he had given up.

I saw that younger brother colour up to the roots of his bright hair as Jaquetta walked up the aisle, in her drawn black silk bonnet with the pink lining (made by herself); and I think she coloured too, for she was rosier than usual when we faced round in the corners of our pew.

We saw no more of them for a month, and a dainty, bridal-looking little lady appeared in the parsonage seat, with white ribbons in her straw bonnet, and modest little orange flowers in the frill round her pleasant face.

Mrs. Cradock she was, we heard; and not only Miss Prior, but Fulk, wanted us to call on her.

"What's the use?" said I. "Farmers' families are not on visiting terms with the ladies of the parsonage."

Poor Jaquey uttered an "Oh dear!" but she and Fulk knew I was past moving in that mood.

However, one morning in the next week, in walked Fulk into the keeping-room, and the clergyman with him, and found Jaquey and me standing at the long table under the window, peeling and cutting up apples for apple-cheese.

"Mr. Cradock, my sister," he said, just in the old tone when he brought a friend into our St. James's-street drawing-room; and he hardly gave time for the shaking of hands before he had returned to the discussion about the change of ministry, just with the voice and animation I had not seen for two whole years.

We went on with our apples. For one thing, we were not wanted; for another, there was no fire in the little parlour, and the gentlemen both seemed to be enjoying the bright one that was burning on the hearth.

The only difficulty was that dinner time began to approach. The men could not be kept waiting; and I heard Alured awake from his sleep, pattering about and shouting; and as we began to gather up our apples one of the maids peeped in with a table-cloth over her arm.

Mr. Cradock saw, though Fulk did not, and said his wife would expect him; and then he looked most pleasantly to me, and said he was not at all wanted at home, while his wife was luxuriating in a settlement of furniture; but this was, he was assured, the last day of confusion, and to-morrow she would be quite ready for all who would be so good as to call on her.

I could only say I would do myself the pleasure; and then he still waited a moment to say that his brother Arthur could not recover from his dismay at his greeting to Miss Torwood.

"But," he said, "the boy's head was quite turned by the beauty of the country. He had been raving all day about the new poet, Alfred Tennyson, and I believe he thought he had walked into lotus-land."

"Nearer the dragon of the Hesperides, perhaps," said Fulk, laughing. "Is he with you now?"

"No; he has gone back to Oxford. He is in his second year; and whether he takes to medicine or to art is to be settled by common-sense or genius."

"Oh, but if he has genius?" began Jaquetta eagerly.

"That's the question," said Mr. Cradock, laughing. "But I am hindering you shamefully," and with that he took his leave, having quite demolished our barriers.

And his wife was of the same nature—simple, blithe, and bonny—ready to make friends in a moment; and though she must have known all about us, never seeming to remember anything but that we were her nearest lady neighbours.

Jaquetta, whose young friendships had been broken short off, because the poor girls really did not know how to correspond with her under present circumstances, took to Mrs. Cradock with eager enthusiasm, and tripped across the park to her two or three times a week, and became delightedly interested in all her doings, parochial or otherwise.

Dear Jaquey's happy nature had always been content; but when I saw how exceedingly she enjoyed the variety, liveliness, and occupations brought by the Cradocks, I felt that it had been scarcely kind to seclude her to gratify my own sole pride; but then there had been nobody like the Cradocks—to drop or be dropped.

The refreshment to Fulk was even greater. The having a man to converse with, and break his mind against, one who would argue, and who really cared for the true principles of politics, made an immense difference to him. When after tea he said he would walk to the parsonage to see how the debate had gone, and we knew we should not see him till half-past ten, we could not but be glad; it must have been so much pleasanter than playing at chess, listening to our old music, or reading even the new books they lent us.

He brightened greatly that winter, and I ceased to fear that he was getting a farmer's slouch. He looked as stately and beautiful as ever Lord Torwood had done, and the dejection had gone out of his face and bearing, when suddenly it returned again; and as Miss Prior was away from home, I never found out the cause till one day, as I was shopping at Shinglebay, and was telling the linen draper that Mr. Torwood would call for the parcel, I saw the lady at the other counter start and turn round, as if at a sudden shock.

Then I saw the white doe eyes, full of the old pleading expression, and the lips quivering wistfully, but I only said to myself, "The old arts! That is what has overthrown Fulk again;" and away I went with a rigid bow, and said nothing.

There was no exchange of calls. That was not my fault, for we could not have begun; and we heard that Mrs. Deerhurst said, "The Torwoods had shown very good taste in retiring from all society, poor things. Only it was a great mistake to remain in the neighbourhood—so awkward for everybody!"

Mrs. Cradock was much struck with Emily's sweet looks; but I believe that Jaquetta told her all about it, and we never met the Deerhursts there.

In fact they were not intimate, for there must have been a repulsion between Mrs. Deerhurst and such a woman as Mary Cradock.

The Deerhursts owned a villa on the outskirts of Shinglebay; indeed, I believe it was the difficulty in letting it that had unwillingly forced Mrs. Deerhurst home, after having married her second daughter, but not Emily. She was only a mile and a half from Spinney Lawn, and speedily became familiar there, being as entirely Hester's counsellor in etiquette as was Perrault on business. People saw a marked improvement in elegance from the time she became adviser.

That next winter poor Joel Lea died. I suppose it was merely the dulness and want of exercise that killed him, for he had lost flesh and grown languid in manner for months before a low fever set in, and he had no power to struggle with it.

He had been ill a long time, when he sent a message to beg Mr. Torwood to come and see him. Jaquetta and I persuaded ourselves that he had discovered that Perrault had suborned witnesses, or done something that would falsify the whole trial.

Jaquetta said she should be very glad for Fulk, and if it happened now little Alured would never feel it; but for her own part, she should hate to go back to be my lady again. She had never known before what happiness was.

I could not help laughing. Nobody had ever detected anything amiss with Lady Jaquetta Trevor's spirits, but that they were too high at times.

"Of course I don't mean that I was miserable!" she said; "but there's something now that does make everything so delicious."

"Could you not take that something to the park?" I asked, laughing.

"I don't know! It would not be so bad if I could run in and out at the parsonage as I do now."

And as I smiled, it smote me as I recollected that Arthur Cradock was always at the parsonage in the vacations. Jaquetta had been sketched many a time as nymph of the orchard, and many a nymph besides. And if he was yielding to his brother's wisdom in making medicine his study and art his pleasure, was not our unconscious maiden the sugar that sweetened the cup of prudence? Might not elevation be as sore a trial to her as depression had been to us?

However, our troubling ourselves was all nonsense. Good Joel Lea would never have connived at any evil doings. All he had wanted of Fulk was to be certain of his forgiveness for the injury he had suffered through his wife, and to entreat him to keep a watch over her and the boy.

"You are her brother, when all is come and gone," he said; "and I do not trust that Perrault. If ever he fails her, or turns against her, you'll stand her friend, and look to the boy?"

Fulk heartily promised, and Joel further begged him to write to her eldest brother, Francis Dayman (who was prospering immensely in the timber trade), and let him know the state of things—though he had been so angered at Hester's sacrifice of his mother's good name and his own birth, that he had broken with her entirely.

"But if anyone can get her out of Perrault's hands, it is Francis," poor Joel said; and he went on to talk of his poor boy, about whom he was very anxious, having no trust in any of Hester's intimates, and begging Fulk to throw a good word to him now and then.

"He thinks much of you," he said. "I heard him tell Miss Deerhurst that it was no use for anyone to try to be such an out-and-out gentleman as his uncle, for they couldn't do it, and he had rather be like you than anyone else. I don't care for gentlemen, and all that foolery, as you know. I wish I could leave him to my old mate, Eli Potter; but you are true and honest, Fulk Torwood, and I think not so far from the kingdom—"

Then he asked Fulk to read a chapter to him. No one else would do so, except little Trevor, when now and then left alone with him; but Hester would not believe him seriously ill, and thought the Bible wearied him and made him low spirited; and as to his friend the Dissenter, she would never admit him.

Fulk was so indignant that he wanted to drive to Shinglebay and fetch Mr. Ball, but Lea thanked him and half smiled at his superstition of thinking that a minister was needed to speed his soul; but he was pleased that Fulk came to him on each of the four or five remaining days of his life, and read to him whatever he wished.

He sank suddenly at last, while Hester was at church on Sunday morning, and died when alone with Fulk.

Somehow the intense reality of that man and the true comfort his faith was to him made an immense impression on my brother, and seemed, as it were, to give the communication between his religious belief and his feelings, which had somehow not been in force before. He thought and borrowed books from Mr. Cradock, and there came a deepening and softening over him, which one saw in many ways, that made him dearer than ever. He looked more at peace, even though one felt that each passing sight of Emily was a sting.

Hester was dreadfully stricken down at first, and her anguish of lamentation and self-reproach was terrible to witness; but she would not hear of Fulk's fetching either of us—indeed, I fancy that was the fault of my dry, cold looks—nor would she allow him to do anything for her.

Mrs. Deerhurst came to be with her, and Perrault managed everything.

They had a magnificent funeral—much grander than my father's—and laid him in the family vault.

Perrault took the opportunity of insulting Fulk by pairing him with old Hall, the ex-agent; but Hall found it out in time, and refused to go, and when the moment came everybody fell back, and Fulk found himself close to poor little Trevor, who tried to get his hand out of Perrault's and cling to him; but Perrault held him tight till, at the moment when they moved to the mouth of the vault and were to go down the steps, terror completely seized the poor child, and he began to shriek so fearfully that Fulk had to snatch him up and carry him out of the church, trembling from head to foot.

It was very cruel to send a sensitive child of six years old in that way; but Hester was too much exhausted with her violent grief to go herself, and, devoted mother as she was in all else, she never perceived that poor child's instinctive shrinking from Perrault.

We tried to be kind to her, and hoped she would soften towards us; but she did not. I could see her eyes glitter with their keen, searching glance under her crape veil, as if she were measuring Alured all over when the child walked into church with me; and, indeed, when he went to the Zoological Gardens some time later, and saw the cobra di capello, he said—

"Ursa, why does that snake look at me just like Lady Hester?"

There must have been fascination in the eager mystery of the gaze, for, strangely enough, he was not afraid of her. She always made much of him if he came in her way, and he was so fond of Trevor Lea that nothing made him so eager or happy as the thought of seeing him.

The one idea that her boy was ousted by Alured, and the longing to see him the heir, seemed to drive out everything else from Hester—almost feeling for her husband.

Fulk had written to Francis Dayman, and he intended to come and see after his sister as soon as he could leave his business; but this rather precipitated matters. Hester was persuaded that Alured could not live through that eighth year of his life at the utmost, and Perrault somehow persuaded her, that only as her husband could he protect her interests and Trevor's, though what machinations she could have expected from us, I cannot guess; or how, in the case of a minor, we could have interfered with her rights. But the man had gained such an ascendancy over her, that she did not even perceive that the connection was not good for that great object of hers, her son's position in society. In fact, he persuaded her that he was of a noble old French family, and ought to be a count. How we laughed when we heard of it! She did preserve wisdom enough to insist upon having her fortune conveyed to trustees for her son, so that Perrault could only touch the income, and not the principal; and as she told everyone that he had been determined upon this being done, I suppose he saw that any demur would excite her suspicion.

They went to London, and were married there, while we were still scouting poor Miss Prior's rumours. We were very sorry when we thought of poor Joel's charge; and, besides, "the count" had an uncomfortable slippery look about him. I can't describe it otherwise. He was a slim, trim, well-dressed man, only given to elaborate jewellery and waistcoats, with polished black hair and boots, and keen French-looking eyes, well-mannered, and so versatile and polite, that he soon overcame people's prejudices; and he was thought to make a much better master of the house than poor Joel had ever done.

CHAPTER VI.

THE WHITE DOE'S WARNING.

Here was Alured's eighth birthday, and he had never been ill at all, but was as fine-looking healthy a boy as could be seen.

We took him to London, and showed him to Dr. Hart, and he said that the old tendency was entirely outgrown, and that Lord Trevorsham was as likely to live and thrive as any child of his age in England.

It really seemed the beginning of a new life, not to have that dreadful fear hanging over us any longer! We felt settled, that was one thing; not as if we should do as Bertram expected, have to come off to New Zealand.

The farm had just began to pay. Fulk's sales of cattle had been, for the first time, more than enough to clear his rent. He had a great ox in the Smithfield Cattle Show, and met our Lupton uncles there not as an unsuccessful man.

And I? I had a dim feeling that Alured would soon cease to need me, and Jaquetta would not be claimed for a long time; and if—

But in the midst of that I saw a haggard face driving in the park by the side of a little, over-dressed, faded woman.

And Aunt Amelia told me how (in the rebound from my harshness, no doubt) Mr. Decies had, as it were, dropped into the hands of a weak, extravagant girl, who had long been using all the intellect she had to attract him, and now led him a dreary life of perpetual dissipation.

I don't know how much I had been to blame. I am sure he was meant for better things. Mine could never have been real love for him, and the refusal could not have been wrong. It must have been the pride and harshness that stung him!

I was very sorry for him, though I could not think about it, of course, still less speak; but that was the beginning of my hating myself, and I have hated myself more and more ever since I have taken to write all this down, and seen how hard and foolish I was, how very much the worst of the three.

Even my care for Alured sprang out of exclusive passion, and so, though I do think that by Heaven's mercy I had a great share in cherishing him into strength and health, I had managed him badly, I had indulged him over much, and was improperly resentful of any attempt of Jaquetta, or even of Fulk, to interfere with him or restrain him.

Thus, when the anxiety was over, and he was a strong boy, full of health and activity, his will was entirely unrestrained, he had no notion of minding any of us, still less of learning. Trevor Lea could read, write, talk French, say a few Latin declensions, when Alured could not read a word of three letters, and would not try to learn.

Oh! the antics he played when I tried to teach him! Then Fulk tried, and he was tame for three days, but then came idleness, wilfulness, anger, punishment, but he laughed to scorn all that we could find in our hearts to do to him.

As to getting other help we were ashamed till he should be a little less shamefully backward. The Cradocks offered to teach him, but then, unless he was elaborately put on honour, he played truant.

He had plenty of honour, plenty of affection, but not the smallest conscience as to obedience; and Fulk would not have the other two motives worked too hard, saying the one might break, the other give way.

We had not taught obedience, so we had to take the consequences, and we were the less able to enforce it that he had come to a knowledge of our mutual relations much sooner than we intended, and in the worst manner possible.

Of course he knew himself to be Lord Trevorsham, and owner of the property; but one day, when Fulk found him galloping his pony in the field laid up for hay, and ordered him out, he retorted that "You ain't my proper brother, and you haven't any rights over me! It is my field; and I shall do as I like."

Fulk got hold of the pony's bridle, and took Alured by the shoulder without one word, then took him into the little study, and had it out with him.

It was Hester who had told him. He had been at Spinney Lawn with Trevor all one afternoon, when we had thought him out with old Sisson. He had told no falsehood indeed, but Hester and her husband had made him understand, so far as such a child could do, that there was some disgrace connected with us; that Fulk had once been in his place, and only wanted to get it back, and now had it all his own way with his young lordship's property, and that he owed us neither duty nor affection, only to his true relative, Lady Hester Perrault.

The dear boy had maintained stoutly that he did love Ursula and Jacquey, and that Hester wasn't half so nice, and that he had rather they bullied him than that she coaxed him! But there was the poison sown—to rankle and grow and burst out when he was opposed. He had full faith and trust in Fulk, and accepted his history, owning, indeed, from a boy, that he had been a horrid little wretch for saying what he did, and asking whether it had not been a great bore; indeed, he behaved all the better instead of the worse for some little time, dear fellow.

But he was too big and strong to tie to one's apron-string, and his greatest pleasure was in being with Trevor. I think Trevor's own influence never did any harm. Poor Joel Lea had trained him well, and he was a conscientious, good boy, who often hindered Alured from insubordination; but the attraction to Spinney Lawn was a mischievous thing—for there was no doubt that the heads of the family would set him against us if they could.

So Fulk thought it wiser to send him to school, since he was learning nothing properly at home, and only getting more disobedient and unruly.

Immediately Trevor Lea was sent to the same school, to the boys' great delight. They cared little that Trevor was placed nearly at the top and

Trevorsham at the bottom of the little preparatory school. They held together just as much, and Alured came home wonderfully improved and delightfully good, but more than ever inseparable from Trevor.

In the meantime Francis Dayman had come to pay his sister a visit. He had made some fortunate speculations, and had come on to be a merchant of considerable wealth and weight in the Hudson's Bay Company.

A handsome man of a good deal of strength and force he seemed to be, and Perrault had certainly been wise in securing his prize before Hester had such a guardian.

He was an open, straight-forward man, with a fresh breath of the forest about him; successful beyond all his hopes, and full of activity. He took to Fulk, and seemed to have a strong fellow-feeling for us.

But little had Fulk expected to be made the confidant of his vehement admiration for Emily Deerhurst. The gentle lady-like girl impressed the backwoodsman in a wondrous manner. It seemed to him, as if his wealth would have real value, if he could pour it all out on her.

And her mother encouraged him. Emily was six years older than when she had cast off Fulk, and there was a pale changed look about her; and the rich Canadian, who could buy a baronetcy, and do anything she asked, tempted Mrs. Deerhurst.

Though, as Fulk said bitterly, if the stain on his birth was all the cause of the utter withdrawal, was it not the same with Francis Dayman? Only in his case it was gilded!

Dayman knew nothing of this former affair. The world was forgetting it, and if Hester knew it, she kept it from his knowledge, so he used to consult Fulk as to what was to be done to please an English lady, and whether he was too rough for her; and Fulk stood it all. He even knew when the young lady herself was brought forward—and refused, gently, sadly, courteously, but unmistakably; and then, when driven hard by the eager wooing, owned to an old attachment, that never would permit her to marry!

What a light there was in Fulk's eyes when he whispered that into my ears! And yet he had kept his counsel, even though Mr. Dayman told him that the mother declared it to be a foolish romantic affair of very early girlhood, that no doubt his perseverance would overthrow.

"And her persecution!" muttered poor Fulk. But he did enjoy the confidences in a bitter-sweet fashion. It was justifiable to be a dog in the manger under the circumstances.

Mr. Dayman went to London, and Hester was negotiating about a house where Mrs. Deerhurst and her daughters were to stay with her for a few weeks. I fancy Mrs. Deerhurst thought that the chance of seeing Farmer Torwood ride by to market had a bad effect. It was the Easter holidays, and both boys were at home; always trying to be together, and we not finding it easy to keep Alured from Spinney Lawn, without such flat refusals as would have given his sister legitimate cause of complaint and offence.

One beautiful spring afternoon, when Alured, to my vexation and vague uneasiness, had gone over there, I was sowing annuals in the garden and watching for him at the same time, when, to my surprise, I saw, coming over the fields from the park, a lady with a quick, timid, yet wearied step. Had she lost her way, I thought? There was something of the tame fawn in her movement; and then I remembered the white doe. Yes! it was Emily!

The one haunting anxiety of my life broke out—"You haven't come to say there's anything amiss with my boy?" I cried out.

"No; oh no! I think he is safe now; but I wanted to tell you, I think you ought to be warned."

She was trembling so much that I wanted to bring her in and make her rest; but she would only sit down on the step of the stile, and there she whispered it, in this way.

"You know there's a dreadful scarlet fever at old Brown's."

"The old man that sells curiosities? No, I did not know it; I'll keep Trevorsham away," I said, wondering she had come all this way; and then asking in a fright, "Surely he has not been there?"

"No; I met him on the road with Lady Hester Perrault, and I told them. I walked back to Spinney Lawn with them. But," as I began to thank her, and her voice went lower still, "but—oh, Ursula, Lady Hester knew it!"

"Knew it!"

"Yes, knew it quite well."

"She was doing it on purpose!"

"Oh," Emily hid her face in her hands, "I pray God to forgive me if I am doing a very cruel wicked wrong; but I can't help thinking it. I had told her only yesterday how bad the fever was in that street. She said she had forgotten it, and thanked me; but she had not her own boy, Trevor, with her."

I was too much frozen with the horror of the thing to speak at first, and perhaps Emily thought I did not quite believe her, for she said, under her breath, "And I've heard her talk—talk to mamma—about her being so certain that Lord Trevorsham could not live, even when he was past seven years old. They always have said that the first illness would go to his head and carry him off. And when people do wish things very much—" And then she grew frightened at herself, and began blaming herself for the horrible fancy, but saying it haunted her every time she saw Lord Trevorsham in Lady Hester's sight. That old ballad, "The wee grovelling doo," would come into her head, and she had felt as if any harm happened to the child it would be her fault for not having spoken a word of warning, and this had determined her.

By this time I had taken it in, and then the first thing I did was to spring up and ask how she could leave the boy still in the woman's power, to which she answered that she had walked them back to Spinney Lawn—a whole mile— and that Lady Hester could not set forth again, now that Alured had heard the conversation.

He had been bent on going to buy a tame sea-gull there, as a birthday present for Trevor; and Emily had lured him off from that, by a promise of getting one from an old fisherman whom she knew. So there was not much fear of his running back into the danger, though I should not have a happy moment till he was in my sight again.

Then Emily sprang up, saying, she must go. She had walked four miles, and she must get back as fast as she could. Most likely mamma would think her at Spinney Lawn.

But what must not it have cost that timid thing to venture here with her warning!

It gave me a double sense of the reality of my boy's, peril, that she had been excited to it, and she would not hear of coming in to rest; and when I entreated her to wait till I could get the gig to drive her part of the way, she held me fast, and insisted, with all the terror of womanly shamefacedness, that, "he—that Tor—that Mr. Torwood—should not know." And she sprang up to go home instantly, before he could guess.

"Oh, Emily, that is too bad, when nothing would make him so glad."

"Oh! no, no! he has been used too ill; he can't care for me now, and as if I should—"

I don't think poor Emily uttered anything half so coherent as this, at any rate I understood that she disclaimed the least possibility of his affection continuing, and felt it an outrage on herself to be where she could even suppose herself to have voluntarily put herself in his way.

I thought there was nothing for it but to let her start, hurry after her with some vehicle, and then call and bring home my boy; but in the midst of my perplexity and her struggle with her tears, who should appear on the scene but Fulk himself, driving home the spring cart wherein, everybody being busy, he had conveyed a pig to a new home.

I don't know how it was all done or said. My first notion was that he should be warned of our dear boy's danger, and rescue him before anything else. I could not get into my head that there was no present reason for dread, and yet when I had gasped out "Oh, Fulk—Alured—Fetch him home! Emily came to warn us!" the accusation began to seem so monstrous and horrible that I could not go on with it before Emily. She too, perhaps, found it harder to utter to a man than to a woman, and between the strangeness of speaking to one another again, and her shyness and his wonder and delight, it seemed to me unreasonable that poor little Alured's danger was counting for nothing between them, and I turned from the former reticence to the bereaved tigress style, and burst out, "And are we to stand talking here while our boy is in these people's power?"

Then Fulk did listen to what it was all about; but even then it seemed to me he would not think half so much of the peril as of what Emily had done. In truth, I believe all they both wanted was to get out of my way; but they pacified me by Fulk's undertaking, if Emily did not object to the cart, to drive her across the park where no one would meet her, and she could get out only a mile from home, and to call at Spinney Lawn in returning by the road and take up Alured.

What a drive that must have been! Fulk had the advantage over Emily in knowing what poor Mr. Dayman had told him, whereas she, poor child, only knew that he had been so vilely served that she thought his affection and esteem had been entirely killed.

They had it all out in that tax cart, a vehicle Fulk now regards as a heavenly chariot, and I heard it all afterwards.

Poor Emily! she had grown a great deal older in those six years. At eighteen she had implicitly believed in her mother. Mrs. Deerhurst had been so good all those years of striving not to frighten my father, that she had been perfection in her daughter's eyes. Emily had believed with all her heart in her apparent disinterestedness, and her hopes and sympathy for us were real; and so, when the crash really came, and she told the poor girl with floods of tears that it was impossible, and a thing not to be thought of, for a right-minded woman to unite herself to a man of such birth. And poor Emily, with the conscious ignorance of eighteen, believed, and was the sort of gentle creature who could easily be daunted by the terror that her generous impulses to share the shame and namelessness were unfeminine and wrong. The utter silence had been the consequence of her mother assuring her, with authority, that the true kindness was to betray no token of feeling that could cherish hope where all was hopeless, and that he would regret her less if she commanded herself and gave him no look.

It had been terrible, calm self-command, and obedience to abused filial confidence in her mother's infallibility.

And then Mrs. Deerhurst had been sinking ever since in her daughter's esteem, as Emily could not but rise higher from the conscientious struggle and self-denying submission, and besides grew older and had more experience; while Mrs. Deerhurst, no doubt, deteriorated in the foreign wandering life, and all her motives made themselves evident when she married the younger daughter.

Emily had thought for herself, and seen that advantage had been taken of her innocence, and that her betrothed had rights, which, if she had been older, she would not have been persuaded to ignore. But coming home, two years later, and meeting my cold eyes and Fulk's ceremonious bow, and hearing on all parts that he had accepted his position and had a hard struggle to maintain his two sisters; she, knowing herself to be portionless, could but suffer, and be still.

Of course every attempt of her mother's to get her to marry advantageously, and, even more, Mrs. Deerhurst's devotion to Lady Hester, tore away more and more of the veil she had tried to keep over her eyes; and as her youngest sister grew up into bloom, and into the wish for society, Emily had been allowed more and more to go her own quiet way in the religious and charitable life of Shinglebay, where she had peace, if not joy.

And then came the Dayman affair, when all the old persecution revived again, and Emily's foremost defence against him, her blushing objection to his birth, was set aside as a mere prudish fancy of a young girl.

The gentle Emily had been irate then, and all the more when her mother tried to cover her inconsistency by alleging that everybody knew of Lord Torwood's fall, whereas no one knew or cared who Francis Dayman was, or where he came from. Henceforth Emily's shame at the usage of Fulk had been double—or rather it turned into indignation. Reports that he was to marry a rich grazier's daughter had no effect in turning her in pique to Dayman. She had firmly told her mother that if it were wrong for her to take the one, it must be equally so to take the other.

This Mrs. Deerhurst had concealed from poor Mr. Dayman; nor would Emily's modesty allow her to utter the objection to the man's own face. So Mrs. Deerhurst encouraged him, and trusted to London reports of the grazier's daughter, and persevering appeals to that filial sense of duty which had been strained so much too far.

And now, how did it stand?

When I, secure in knowing that Alured was safe at home, thinking it abominable nonsense in Miss Deerhurst to have bothered about scarlet fever, Hester herself had said so. When I could hear Fulk's happiness, and try to analyse it, what did it amount to?

Why, that they knew they loved one another still, and never meant to cease. And with what hopes? Alas! the hopes were all for some time or other. Emily would do nothing in flat disobedience, and there was little or no hope of her mother's consent to her marrying Farmer Torwood. She meant to tell her mother thus much, that she had seen him, and that they loved each other as much as ever; and as Mrs. Deerhurst had waived the objection to Dayman, it could not hold in the other case. It would be, in fact, a tacit compact— scarcely an engagement—with what amount of meeting or correspondence must be left for duty and principle to decide, but the love that had existed without aliment for six years might trust now. And "hap what hap," there never was a happier man than my Fulk that evening.

He was too joyous not to be universally charitable. Nay, he called it a blessed fancy of Emily's that brought her here, as it was Emily's, and had brought him such bliss he could not quite scorn it, but he did not, *could* not believe in it as we did. It was culpable carelessness in Hester, but colonial people had been used to such health that they did not care about infection. But it was a glorious act of Emily's! In fact the manly mind could believe nothing so horrible of any woman.

CHAPTER VII.

HUNTING.

Emily told Mr. Dayman the whole truth. Poor fellow! he could not face Fulk again, and went back to Canada.

No doubt Emily went through a great deal, but we never exactly knew what.

Fulk wrote to Mrs. Deerhurst, stating that he hoped in four years' time to be able to purchase the farm, of which he had the lease, and without going into the past, asking her sanction to the engagement.

She sent a cold letter in answer, to desire that the impertinence should not be repeated.

And Emily wrote that her mother would not hear of the engagement, and she knew Fulk would not wish her to deceive or disobey, "And so we must trust one another still; but how sweet to do that!"

And when any of us met her there were precious little words and looks, and Fulk meant to try again after the four years. In the meantime he was much respected, and had made himself a place of his own. It chafed Hester to perceive that though she had pulled us down she could not depress us after the first. She had lowered her position, too, by her marriage. At first Perrault was on his good behaviour, and made a favourable impression among the second-rate Shinglebay society Hester got round her; but as the hopes of the title coming to her diminished, he kept less within bounds, did not treat her well at home, and took to racing and gambling.

I never could get Fulk to share my alarms about Alured, but he did not think Perrault's society fit for the boy, told Alured so, and forbade him to go to Spinney Lawn. But though Alured was much improved as to obedience, it was almost impossible to enforce this command. Hester had some strange fascination for him. She would fiercely caress him at times, and he knew she was his sister, and could not see why, when she was often alone, he should not be with her. The passion for Trevor was in full force, too, and the boys could not be content only to meet at the farm. We tried sending Alured to make visits from home in the holidays, but he did not like it, and he was not happy; his heart was with his home, and with Trevor. We tried having a tutor for the spring holidays before he went to Eton, but it did not answer. He was not a sensible man, did not like dining in the keeping-room with the household, and though he did it, he showed that he thought it a condescension.

Moreover, instead of attending to Alured, he was always trying to flirt with Jaquetta, infinitely disturbing Arthur Cradock's peace; and the end of it was, that Alured was a great deal more left to his own devices than ever he had been before, and exasperated besides.

He was in that mood, when one day, as he was riding along the lanes, he met Perrault and Trevor coming in from hunting.

Alured had a very pretty pony, but he was growing rather large for it, and Fulk had promised that, if he worked well at Eton, he should have a lovely little Arab, that was being trained by a dealer he knew; and that another year, Fulk himself would go out hunting with him.

Perrault began to pity him for having missed the run. Why did not his brother take him out? Fulk's old mare was a sort of elephant, and it was not convenient to get another horse just then. That Alured knew and explained, but he was pitied the more for being kept back, and Perrault ended by saying that if on the next hunting day he could meet them at the corner of the park, a capital mount should be there for him.

The hour was attainable if Alured made haste with his studies, and he accepted gladly, and without compunction. Fulk had never in so many words forbidden him, and besides, Fulk had delegated his authority to the hateful tutor.

But the next morning, before Alured was up Trevor was in his bedroom. "You won't go, Trevorsham?"

"Yes, I shall; I'm not such a muff as to stay for that fellow."

But I need not try to tell what passed, as of course I did not hear it; I never so much as knew of it till long after, only Trevorsham was determined, and Trevor tried all round the due arguments of principle, honour, and duty; but Alured had worked up a schoolboy self-justification on all points, and besides had the stronghold of "I will," and "I don't care."

Then Trevor told him, under his breath, he was sure it was not a safe horse. But my high-spirited boy laughed this to scorn. "And perhaps he'll play you some trick," added Trevor. But Trevorsham was still undaunted in his self-will, till Trevor resolutely announced his determination, if nothing else would stop it, of going at once to Fulk, and informing him.

The boy endured all the rage and scorn that a threat so contrary to all schoolboy codes of honour and friendship might deserve. I believe Alured struck him, but at any rate Trevor Lea gained his point, though at the cost of a desperate quarrel.

Alured held aloof and sulked at him for the remaining fortnight at home, and only vouchsafed the explanation to us that "Lea was a horrid little sneak, and he had done with him."

They did not make it up till they met in the same house at Eton, and then, though Trevor was placed far above Alured, they became as friendly as ever. In fact, I believe, Alured, having imprudently denominated himself by his full title, was having it kicked out of him, when the fortunate possessor of the monosyllabic name came and stood by him and made common cause, to the entire renewing of love.

Poor Trevor! his was a dreary home. His mother loved him passionately, but she was an anxious, worn, disappointed woman, always craving, restless and expectant of something, and Perrault was always tormenting her for money. He was deeply in debt, and though he could not touch the bulk of her fortune—neither, indeed, could she, as it was conveyed to trustees—he was always demanding money of her, and bullying her; while matters grew worse and worse, and they were in danger of having to let Spinney Lawn and go to live abroad.

As to keeping Trevor at Eton that was becoming impossible. At Christmas the tutor consulted Fulk about how he should get Lea's bills paid, and intimated that he must not return unless this were done.

And poor Trevor himself had little comfort except with us. We encouraged him to come to us, for we had all come to have a very real love for the dear lad himself, and we saw he was unhappy at home; besides that, it was the only way of keeping Alured contented.

Trevor had entirely left off inviting Alured to Spinney Lawn. Partly, he was too gentlemanly and good a boy not to be ashamed of the men who hung about the stables; and besides, we now perceive that the same awful impression that was on Emily Deerhurst was upon him, and that he had a sense that Trevorsham was regarded in a manner that made his presence there a peril.

He was but a boy, and it was an undefined horror, and he never breathed a word of it; but oh, there was a weight on that young brow, an anxious look about the face, and though now and then he would be all joy and fun, still there was the older, more sorrowful look about him.

We thought he was grieving at not going back to Eton, and Fulk was living in hopes of an answer to the letter he had written to Francis Dayman about it, but that was not all. One day—Christmas Eve it was—Mr. Cradock, on coming into the church to look at the holly wreaths, found Trevor kneeling on his father's gravestone in the pavement, sobbing as if his heart was breaking, and heard between the sobs a broken prayer about "Forgive"—"don't let them do it"—"turn mother's heart."

Then Mr. Cradock went out of hearing, but he waited for the boy outside, and asked if he could do anything for him.

"No." Trevor shook his head, thanked him, and grew reserved.

CHAPTER VIII.

DUCK SHOOTING.

Alured's thirteenth birthday was on the 10th of January, and he had extracted a promise from Fulk, to take him duck-shooting to the mouth of our little river.

Nothing can be prettier than our tide river by day, with the retreating banks overhung with trees, the long-legged herons standing in the firs, looking like toys in a German box; while the breadth of blue water reflects the trees that bend down to it.

But, on a winter's night, to creep in perfect silence and lie still under an overhanging bank, not daring to make a sound, till you could get a shot at the ducks disporting themselves in the moonlight, on the frozen mud on the banks! Such an occupation could only be endurable under the name of sport.

However, Fulk and Bertram had had their time, and now Alured was having the infection in his turn; but Trevor was driven over to spend the day, much mortified that he had a bad broken chilblain, which made his boots unwearable, and it was the more disappointing, that it was a very hard frost, and there was a report that some wild swans had been seen on the river.

But in the course of the day Jaquetta routed out a pair of India rubber boots which, with worsted stockings beneath, did not press the chilblains at all, and after having spent all the day in snow-balling and building forts, Trevor declared himself far from lame, and resolved not to lose the fun. He had not come equipped, so Alured put him into an old grey coat and cap of his own, and merrily they started in the frosty moonlight, with dashes of snow lying under the hedges, and everything intensely light. Fulk grumbling in fun at being dragged away from his warm fire, and pretending to be grown old, the boys shouting to one another full of glee, all the dogs in the yard clamouring because only the wise old retriever, Captain, was allowed to be of the party; Arthur Cradock making ridiculous mistakes on purpose between the uncle and nephew, Trevorsham and Sham Trevor, as he called them.

Alas! Nay, shall I say alas, or only be thankful?

They had been gone some time when we heard a rapid tread coming towards the porch. Something in the very sound thrilled Jaquetta and me at once with dismay. We darted out, and saw Brand, the head gamekeeper in the park.

"Never fear, my lady; thank God," he said, "my lord is quite safe. It is poor

Master Lea who is hurt; and Mr. Torwood sent me up for some brandy, and a mattress, and a lantern, and some cloths."

That assured us that he was alive, and we ran to fulfil the request in the utmost haste, without asking further questions, and sending off Sisson to ride for the poor mother, and to go on to Shinglebay for the doctor, though, to our comfort, we knew that Arthur had almost finished his surgical education, and was sure to know what was to be done.

"A stray shot," we said again and again to each other; and we called Nurse Rowe, and made up a bed in Alured's old nursery, and lighted a fire, and were all ready, with hearts beating heavy with suspense before the steps came back —my poor Alured first, as we held the door open. How pale his face looked! and his brows were drawn with horror, and his steps dragging, saying not a word, but trembling, as he came and held by me, with one hand on my waist, while Fulk and Sisson carried in the mattress, Arthur Cradock at the side, and Perrault, who had joined them, walking behind with the flask.

Dear Trevor lay white with sobbing breath and closed eyes, the cloths and mattress soaked through and through with blood. They put him down on the keeping-room table, and Arthur poured more brandy into his mouth.

I said something of the room being ready but Arthur said very low "He is dying—internal bleeding;" and when Jaquetta asked "Can nothing be done?" he answered, "Nothing but to leave him still."

"Trevorsham," murmured the feeble voice, and Alured was close to him; "Ally! you are all right!" and then again, as Alured assured him he would be better— "No, I shan't; I'm so glad it wasn't you. I always thought he'd do it some day, and now you're quite safe, I want to thank God."

We did not understand those words then; we did soon.

The weak voice rambled on, "to thank God; but oh, it hurts so—I can't—I will when I get there." Then presently "Mother!"

"She'll come very soon," said Alured.

"Mother! oh, mother! Trevorsham, don't let them know. O Trev, promise, promise!"

"Promise what? I promise, whatever it is! Only tell me," entreated Alured.

"Take care of her—of mother. Don't let—" and then his eyes met Perrault's, and a shudder came all over him, which brought the end nearer; and all another spoonful of brandy could do was to enable him to say something in Alured's ear, and then a broken word or two—"forgive—glad— pray;" and when we all knelt and Fulk did say the Lord's Prayer, and a verse or two more, there was a peaceful loving look at Fulk and Jaquetta and me, and then the whisper of the Name that is above every name, as a glad brightness came over the face, and the eyes looked upwards, and so grew set in their gaze, and there was the sound one never can forget.

Nurse Rowe laid her hand on Alured's neck, as he knelt with his head close to Trevor's. Fulk and I looked at each other, and we knew that all was over.

They had tried in vain to check the bleeding. No one could have done more than Arthur had done, but a main artery had been injured, and nothing could have saved him. He had said nothing after the first cry, except when he saw Alured's grief. "Never mind; I'm glad it was not you." And once or twice, as they carried him home, he had begged to be put down, though they durst not attend to the entreaty, and Arthur did not think he had suffered much pain.

It jarred that just as we would have knelt for one silent prayer, Perrault's voice broke on us. "Ah! poor boy, it is better than if it lasted longer! I saw that half-witted fellow, Billy Blake about. So I don't wonder at anything; but of course it was a mere accident, and I shall not press it."

Scarcely hearing him, I had joined Mrs. Rowe in the endeavour to detach Alured from his dear companion, when there was poor Hester among us, with open horror-stricken eyes, and a wild, frightful shriek as she leapt forward; and no words can describe the misery of her voice as she called on her boy to look at her, and speak to her—gathering him into her bosom with a passionate, desperate clasp, that seemed almost an outrage on the calm awful stillness of the innocent child; and Alured involuntarily cried, "Oh, don't," while Fulk spoke to her kindly; but just then she saw her husband, and sprang on her feet, her eyes flashing, her hands stretched out, while she screamed out, "You here? You dare to come here? You, who killed him!" Fulk caught her arm, saying, "Hush! Hester; come away. It was a lamentable accident, but —"

"Oh!" the laugh she gave was the most horrible thing I ever heard. "Accident! I tell you it has been his one thought to make accidents for Trevorsham! And he hated my child—my dear, noble, beautiful, only one! He made him miserable, and murdered him at last!"

She gave another passionate kiss to the cheeks, and then just as I hoped she was going to let us lead her away, she darted from us, rushed past Mr. Cradock who was entering the porch, and in another moment, he hurrying after her, saw her rush down the steep grassy slope, and fling herself into the swollen rapid stream.

His shout brought them all out, and Fulk found him too in the river, holding her, and struggling with the stream, which winter had made full and violent, and the black darkness of the shadows made it hard to find any landing place, and he was nearly swept away before it was possible to get them out of the river; and Fulk was as completely drenched as he was when they brought poor Hester, quite unconscious, up to the house, and brought her to the room that had been prepared for her son; and there Dr. Brown and Arthur gave us plenty to do in filling hot-water baths and warming flannels, or rubbing the icy hands and feet. Only that constant need of exertion could have borne us through the horror of it all. But it was not over yet. There was a call of "Ursula," and as I ran down, I found Fulk standing at the bottom of the stairs with Alured in his arms looking like death!

"I found him on the parlour sofa, the little window and the escritoire open!" Fulk said breathlessly, "the villain!"

"I'm not hurt," said dear Alured's voice, faintly, but reassuringly, "Oh! put me down, Fulk."

We did put him down on the floor—there was no other place—with his head on my lap, and I found strange voices asking him what Perrault had done to him. "Oh! nothing! 'twasn't that. Yes, he's gone, out by the window."

He swallowed some wine and then sat up, leaning against me as I sat at the bottom of the stairs, quite himself again, and assuring us that he was not hurt; Perrault never touched him—"Threatened you, then," said Fulk.

"No," said Alured, as if he hadn't spirit to be indignant; "I meant him to get off."

"Lord Trevorsham!" cried a voice in great displeasure, and I saw that Mr. Halsted, the nearest magistrate, was standing over us.

"He told me—Trevor did"—said Alured.

"Told you to assist the murderer to escape!" exclaimed Mr. Halsted.

Alured let his head fall back, and would not answer, and Fulk said, "There is no need for him to speak at present, is there? The constable and the rest are gone after Perrault, but I do not yet know what has directed the suspicion against him."

And then at the stair foot, for there was no other place to go to, we came to an understanding, the two gentlemen and Brand the keeper standing, and I seated on the step with my boy lying against me. I could not trust him out of my sight, nor, indeed, was he fit to be left.

It seems that Brand had been uneasy about the number of shooters whom the report of the swans had attracted; and though the bank of the river was not Trevorsham ground, he had kept along on the border of the covers higher up the hill, to guard his hares and pheasants.

Thus he had seen everything distinctly in the moonlight against the snowy bank below; and he had observed one figure in particular, moving stealthily along, in a parallel line with that which he knew our party would take, though they were in shadow, and he could not see them.

Suddenly, a chance shot fired somewhere made all the ducks fly up. A head and shoulders that Brand took for his young lord's, appeared beyond the shadow, beside Fulk's; and, at the same moment, he saw the man whom he had been watching level his gun from behind, and fire. Then came the cry, and Brand running down in horror himself, was amazed to see this person doing the same, and when they came up with the group, he recognised Perrault; and found, at the same time, that Trevor was the sufferer, and that Lord Trevorsham was safe. He then would have thought it an accident, but for Perrault's own needless wonder, whence the shot came, and that same remark, that Billy Blake, the half-witted son of a farmer, was about that night.

Brand, a shrewd fellow, restrained his reply, that Mr. Perrault knew most about it himself. He saw that the most pressing need was to obey Fulk in fetching necessaries from our house, and that Perrault meant to disarm suspicion by treating it as an accident, so he thought it best to go off to a magistrate with his story, before giving any alarm; feeling certain, as he said, that the shot had been meant for the Earl; as indeed, Perrault's first exclamation on coming up showed that he too had expected to find Trevorsham the wounded one.

Mr. Halsted had sent for the constable and came at once, though even then inclined to doubt whether Brand had not imputed accident to malice. But Perrault's flight had settled that question. During the confusion, while Hester was being carried upstairs, the miscreant had the opportunity of speaking to the child.

"Drowned! No, she is not drowned; but she may be the other thing if you don't get me off! What, don't you understand? Let the law lay a finger on me, and what is to hinder me from telling how your sweet sister has been plotting to get you—yes, you, out of the way of her darling. No, you needn't fear, there's nothing to get by it now. Lucky for you you brought the poor boy out, when I thought him safe by the fire nursing his chilblain. But mind this, if I am arrested, all the story shall come out. I'll not swing alone. If I fired, she pointed the gun! And you may judge if that was what poor Trevor meant by his mutterings to you about 'mother.'"

"But what do you want?" Alured asked. He had backed up against the wall; he was past being frightened, but he felt numb and sick with horror, and ready to do anything to get the wretch out of his sight.

"I want a clear way out of the house and all the cash you can get together. What! no more than that? I'd not be a lord to be kept so short. Find me some more."

Alured knew I should forgive him, and he took my key from my basket, unlocked the escritoire, and gave him my purse of household money, undid the shutters, and helped Perrault to squeeze himself through the little parlour window; and then, as he said, something came over him, and he just reached the sofa, and knew no more.

He did not tell all this about Hester before Mr. Halsted; only when Fulk, finding how shaken he was, had carried him upstairs, and we had taken him to his room, he asked anxiously whether anyone had heard Hester say that dreadful thing, and added, "Then if Mr. Perrault gets away no one will know —about her."

"Was that why you helped him?" we asked.

"Trevor told me to take care of her," he said; and then he told us of Perrault's arguments, but we ought not to have let him talk of them that night, for it brought back the shuddering and sobbing, and the horror seemed to come upon him, so that there was no soothing him or getting him calm till the doctor mixed an anodyne draught; and let it go as it would with Hester, I never left my boy till I had crooned him to sleep, as in the old times.

CHAPTER IX.

TREVOR'S LEGACY.

Jaquetta bore the brunt of that night, and showed the stuff she was made of, for poor Hester had only revived to fall into a most frightful state of delirium, raving and struggling so that the doctor and Arthur could hardly hold her.

So it went on for hours, Alured the only creature asleep in the house, and we not daring to send for any help from without, poor Hester's exclamations were so dreadful.

Poor Alured! his waking was sad enough! He had loved Trevor with all his heart, and the wonder that anyone could be so wicked oppressed him almost as much as the grief. The remnants of the opiate hung upon him, too, and he lay about all day, hardly rousing himself to speak or look, but giddily and drowsy.

Not till the inquest was it perceived how cleverly Perrault had taken his measures, so that had he not made the mistake between the two boys, he would scarcely have been suspected: certainly not but for Brand's having watched him.

The report of the wild swans was traced to him. No doubt it was as an excuse for a heavier charge, for poor Trevor was wounded with shot that would not have been used merely for ducks, and besides, the other shooters it attracted would be likely to make detection less easy. Indeed, Fulk had seen that there were enough men about to spoil their sport, and but for the boys' eagerness, would have turned back.

Moreover it was proved that Perrault had in the course of the morning met Billy Blake, and asked him if he meant to bag the swan—if he followed the young lord's party and fired when they did, he would be sure to bring something down. He did not know that the Blakes never let the poor fellow load his old gun with anything but powder.

Then his joining the horrified group, as if he had been merely after the ducks, and had been attracted by the cry, had entirely deceived us; and but for Hester's accusation, Brand's evidence, and his own flight, together with all the past, might have continued to do so.

He had gone to his own house, as it afterwards turned out, entered so quietly that the listening, watching servants never heard him, collected all the valuables he could easily carry away, changed his dress, and gone off before the search had followed him thither.

A verdict of wilful murder was returned against him at the inquest, but it is very doubtful whether he could have been convicted of anything but manslaughter; for even if the intention could have been proved, without his wife, whose evidence was inadmissible, the malice was not directed against his victim, but against Trevorsham. We could not but feel it a relief day by day, that nothing was heard of him; for who could tell what disclosures there might be about the poor thing who lay, delirious, needing perpetual watchfulness. Arthur devoted himself to the care of her, and never left us, or I do not see how we could have gone through it all.

Alured was well again, but inert and crushed, and heartless about doing anything, except that he walked over to Spinney Lawn, and brought home

Trevor's dog, to which he gave himself up all day, and insisted on having it in his room at night.

The burial was in the vault—nobody attended but Fulk and Alured, not even Arthur, for though the poor mother was not aware of what was going on, it was such a dreadful day with her, that he durst not leave us alone to the watch. It was enough to break one's heart to stand by the window and hear her wandering on about her Trevor coming to his place, and not being kept from his position; while we watched the little coffin carried across the field by the labouring men, with those two walking after it. Our boy's first funeral was that of the friend who had died in his stead.

We were glad to send him back to Eton, out of the sound of his poor sister's voice; though he went off very mournfully, declaring that he should be even more wretched there without Trevor than he was at home; and that he never should do any good without him. But there he was wrong, I am thankful to say. Dear Trevor was more a guide to him dead than living. Trevor's chief Eton friend, young Maitland, a good, high-principled, clever boy, a little older, who had valued him for what he was, while passing Alured by as a foolish, idle little swell, took pity upon him in the grief and dejection of his loss—did for him all and more than Trevor could do, and has been the friend and blessing of his life, aiding the depth and earnestness that seemed to pass into our dear child as he hung over the dying lad. Yes, Trevor Lea and John Maitland did for our Trevorsham what all our love and care had never been able to do.

Meantime Hester's illness took its course. The chill of that icy water had done great harm, and there was much inflammation at first, leaving such oppression of breath that permanent injury to the lungs was expected, and therefore it was all the sadder to see the dumb despair with which she returned to understanding, I can hardly say to memory, for I believe she had never lost it for a moment.

Hopeless, heedless, reckless, speechless, she was a passive weight, lying or sitting, eating or drinking as she was bidden, but not making any manifestation of preference or dislike, save that she turned rigidly and sullenly away from any attempt to read prayers to her.

She asked no questions, attempted no employment, but seemed to care for nothing, and for weeks uttering nothing but a "yes," "no," or a mechanical "thank you." Jaquetta tried to caress her, by force of nursing and pity. Jaquetta really had come to a warm tender love for her, but she sullenly pushed away the sweet face, and turned aside.

We never ventured to leave her alone, and this, after a time, began to vex her. She bade us go down once or twice, and tried to send away Mrs. Rowe; and at last, when she found it was never permitted, she broke out angrily one day, "You are very absurd to take so much trouble to hinder what cannot make any difference."

It made one's blood run cold, and yet it was a relief that the silence was broken. I can't tell what I said, only I implored her not to think so, and told her that her having been rescued was a sign that Heaven would have her repent and come back, but she laughed that horrible laugh. "Do you think I repent?" she said; "No, only that I left it to that fool! I should have made no mistakes."

I was too much horrified to do anything but hide my eyes and pray. I thought I did not do so obviously, but Hester saw or guessed, stamped at me, and said, "Don't; I will not have it done. It is mockery!"

"Happily you cannot prevent our doing that, my poor Lady Hester," I said.

"All I wish you to do is, what you would do if you had a spark of natural feeling."

"What?" I asked, bewildered at this apparent accusation of unkindness.

"Leave me to myself. Send me from your door. Not oppress me with this ridiculous burthensome care and attention, all out of the family pride you still keep up in the Trevors!" she sneered.

"No, Hester. Sister Hester, will you not believe it is love?" I said, thinking that if she would believe that we loved her and forgave her, it might help her to believe that her Father above did. I had never called her by her name alone before; but I thought it might draw her nearer; but it made her only fiercer.

"Nonsense," she said, "I know better."

And then she fell into the same deadly gloom; but I think she had almost a wild animal's longing for solitude; for she made a solemn promise not to attempt her life if we would only leave her alone!

And we did, though we took care someone was within hearing; for she was still very weak, and we had not a bell in the house, except a little hand one on the table.

So the Easter holidays drew on, and she was still far too weak and unwell for any thought of moving her; so that we were in trouble about Alured's holidays, not liking him to come home to a house of illness that would renew his sorrow, and advising him to accept some invitations from his schoolfellows; but he wrote that he particularly wished to come home—he could not bear to be away, and Maitland wanted to see the place and know all about dear Lea, so might he bring him home?

We were only too glad to consent, and I had gone to sleep with Jaquetta, so as to make room—feeling very happy over the best school report of our boy we had ever had, though not the best we were to have.

He spent two or three days at Mr. Maitland's in London, and then he and his friend, John, came on here.

The railway did not come within twenty miles then, and they had to post from it in flies. How delightful it was to see the tall hat and wide white collar, as he stood up in the open fly, signalling to us, and pointing us out to his friend. Only, what must it have been to the poor sufferer in the room above?

Oh! did not one's heart go out in prayer for her!

Out jumped Alured among all of us, and all the dogs at the garden gate; and the first thing, after his kiss to us all, was to turn to the fly and take out a flower-pot with a beautiful delicate forced rose in it.

"Where's Hester?" he said.

"My dear child, she has not left her room yet."

"She is well enough for me to take this to her, I suppose?" he said. "He always did get some flower like this to bring home to her, you know, she liked them so much."

It was just his one idea that Trevor had told him to take his place to her. We looked doubtfully at each other, but Fulk quietly said, "Yes, you may go." And added, as the boy went off, "It can do no harm to her in the end, poor thing!"

"To her, no; that was not my fear."

There was Alured, almost exactly what Trevor had been when last she saw him, with his bright sweet honest face over the rose, running up the stairs, knocking, and coming in with his boyish, "Good morning, Hester, I do hope you are better;" and bending down with his fresh brotherly kiss on her poor hot forehead, "I've got this rose for you, the bud will be out in a day or two."

If ever there was a modern version of St. Dorothy's roses it was there.

That boy's kiss and his gift touched the place in her heart. She caught him passionately in her arms, and held him till he almost lost breath, and then she held him off from her as vehemently.

"Boy—Trevorsham—what do you come to me for?"

"He told me," said Alured, half dismayed. "Besides, you are my sister."

"Sister, indeed! Don't you know we would have killed you?"

"Never mind that," said Alured, with an odd sort of readiness. "You are my sister all the same, and oh—if you would let me try to be a little bit of Trevor to you, though I know I can't—"

"You—who must hate me?"

"No," said he, "I always did like you, Hester; and I've been thinking about you all the half—whenever I thought of him."

And as the tears came into the boy's eyes, the blessed weeping came at last to Hester.

He thought he had done her harm, for she cried till she was absolutely spent, sick, faint and weak as a child.

But she was like a child, and when her head was on the pillow she begged for Trevorsham to wish her good-night. I think she tried to fancy his kiss was Trevor's.

Any way the bitter black despair was gone from that time. She believed in and accepted his kindness like a sort of after glow from Trevor's love. Perhaps it did her the more good that after all he was only a boy, sometimes forgot her, and sometimes hurried after his own concerns, so that there was more excitement in it than if it had been the steady certain tenderness of an older person on which she could reckon.

She certainly cared for no one like Trevorsham. She even came downstairs that she might see him more constantly, and while he was at home, she seemed to think of no one else. But she had softened to us all, and accepted us as her belongings, in a matter-of-course kind of way. Only when he was gone did she one day say in a heavy dreary tone, that she must soon be leaving us.

But I told her, as we had agreed, that she was very far from well enough to go away alone; for indeed, it was true that disease of the lungs had set in, and to send her away to languish and die alone was not to be thought of.

My answer made her look up to me, and say, "I don't see why you should all be so good to me! Do you know how I have hated you?"

I could not help smiling a little at that, it had so little to do with the matter; but I bent down and kissed her, the first time I had ever done so.

"I don't understand it," she said, and then pushing me away suddenly. "No! you cannot know, that I—I—I was the first to devise mischief against that boy. Perrault would never have thought of it, but for me! Now, you see whom you are harbouring! Perhaps, you thought it all Perrault's doing."

"No, we did not," I said.

"And you still cherish me! I—who drove you from your home and rank, and came from wishing the death of your darling, to contriving it!"

I told her we knew it. And at last, after a long, long silence, she looked up from her joined hands, and said, "If I may only see my child again, even from the other side of the great gulf, I would be ready for any torment! It would be no torment to me, so I saw him! Do you think I shall be allowed, Ursula?"

How I longed for more power, more words to tell her how infinitely more mercy there was than she thought of! I don't think she took it in then, but the beginning was made, and she turned away no more from what she looked on at first as a means of bringing her to her boy, but by-and-by became even more to her.

Gradually she told how the whole history had come about. She had thought nothing of the discovery of her birth till her boy was born, but from that time the one thought of seeing him in the rank she thought his due had eaten into her heart. She had loved her husband before, but his resistance had chafed her, and gradually she felt it an injustice and cruelty, and her love and respect withered away, till she regarded him as an obstacle. And when she had spent her labour on the voyage, and obtained recognition from her father— behold! Alured's existence deprived her of the prize almost within her grasp.

A settled desire for the poor baby's death was the consequence, kept up by the continued reports of his danger. Till that time she had prayed. Then a sense that Heaven was unjust to her and her boy filled her with grim rebellion, and she prayed no more; and Perrault, by his constant return to the subject and speculations on it, kept her mind on it far more.

But Alured lived, and every time she saw him she half hated him, half loved him; hated him as standing in her son's light, loved him because she could not help loving Trevor's shadow.

That day, when Emily met them—it had been a sudden impulse—Alured had been talking to her about his plans for Trevor's birthday; and, as he spoke of that street, the wild thought came over her how easily a fever might yet sweep him away. And yet she says, all down the street, she was trying to persuade herself to forget Emily's warning, and to disbelieve in the infection. After all, she thought, even if she had not met Emily, she should have made some excuse for turning back, such a pitiful thought came of the fair, fresh face flushing and dying.

But it was prevented, only it left fruits; for Perrault had heard what passed between her and Trevorsham. "Did you take him to the shop?" he asked. And when she mentioned Miss Deerhurst's reminder, he said, "Ah! that game wants skill and coolness to carry it out."

She says that was almost all that passed in so many words; but from that time she never doubted that Perrault would take any opportunity of occasioning danger to Trevorsham; and, strange to say, she lived in a continued agony, half of hope, half of terror and grief and pity, her longing for Trevor's promotion, balanced by the thought of the grief he would suffer for his friend. Any time those five years she told me she thought that had she seen Perrault hurting him, she should have rushed between to save him; and yet in other moods, when she planned for her son, she would herself have done anything to sweep Alured from his path.

And the frequent discussion with Perrault of plans depending on the possession of the Trevorsham property, kept the consciousness of his purpose before her, and as debt and desperation grew, she was more and more sure of it.

That last day, when Trevor had been driven away, lamenting his inability to go out duck shooting, Perrault had quietly said in the late evening, "I shall take a turn in the salt marshes to-night—opportunities may offer."

The wretch! Fulk thinks he said so to implicate her.

At any rate it left her shuddering with dread and remorse, yet half triumphant at the notion of putting an end to Fulk's power over the estate, and of installing her son as heir of Trevorsham.

She had no fears for him, she trusted to his lame foot to detain him, and said to herself that if it was to be, he would be spared the sight. She was growing jealous of his love for Alured and of us, and had a fierce glad hope of getting him more to herself.

And then! oh! poor Hester!

No wonder her desire was to be

> Anywhere, anywhere,
> Out of the world.

But out of all the anguish, the remorse, the despair, repentance grew at last. Love seemed to open the heart to it. The sense of infinite redeeming love penetrated at last, and trust in pardon, and with pardon came peace. Peace grew on her, through increasing self-condemnation, and bearing her up as the bodily powers failed more and more.

There is little more to say. She was a dear and precious charge to us, and as she grew weaker, she also became more cheerful! and even that terrible, broken-hearted sense of bereavement calmed.

She found out about Jaquetta and Arthur, and took great interest in his arrangements for getting a partnership at Shinglebay.

"And Hester," said Jaquetta, "it is so lucky for me that I came down from being a fine lady. I might never have known Arthur; and if I had, what an absurd creature I should have been as a poor man's wife!"

As to the Deerhursts, the mother sent a servant once or twice to inquire, but never came herself to see her dear friend; and Miss Prior took care to tell us that there were horrid whispers about, that Hester had known, and if not, Mrs. Deerhurst could not have on her visiting list the wife of a man with a warrant out against him! She thought it very unfeeling in us to harbour her.

But Emily came. Hester had a great longing to thank her for checking her on that walk to the scarlet-fever place, and asked Jaquetta one day to write to her and beg her to come to see a dying woman.

Emily showed the note to her mother, and did not ask leave. The white doe had become a much more valiant animal.

Hester had liked Emily even while Emily shrank from her, and she now realized what she had inflicted upon her and Fulk.

She asked Emily's pardon for it, as she had asked Fulk's, and said that when she was gone she hoped all would come right. Of course the old position could not be restored, but she knew now why Joel Lea had such an instinct against it.

"I feel," she once said, "as if Satan had offered me all this for my soul, and I had taken the bargain. Aye, and if God's providence had allowed our wicked purpose, he would have had it too. My husband! he prayed for me! and my boy did too."

She always called Joel Lea "my husband" now, and thought and talked much of their early love and his warnings. I think the way she had saddened his later years grieved her as much as anything, and all her affection seemed revived.

She lingered on, never leaving the house indeed, but not much worse, till the year had come round again, and we loved her more each day we nursed her. And when the end came suddenly at last, we mourned as for a dear sister.

Perrault wrote once—a threatening, swaggering letter from America, demanding hush-money. It did not come till she was too ill to open it—only in the last week before her death, and it was left till we settled her affairs.

Then Fulk wrote and told him of the verdict against him, and recommended him to let himself be heard of no more. And he took the advice.

We found that dear Hester had left all the fortune, 30,000 pounds, which had been settled on herself and Trevor, to be divided equally between us three. Nor had we any scruple in profiting by it.

Trevorsham had enough, and it was what my father would have given us if he could.

It was enough to make Jaquetta and her young Dr. Cradock settle down happily and prosperously on the practice they bought.

And enough too, together with Emily's strong quiet determination, to make Mrs. Deerhurst withdraw her opposition. Daughters of twenty-nine years old may get their own way.

Moreover a drawing-room and dining-room were built on to Skimping's Lawn, though Alured declares they have spoilt the place, and nothing ever was so jolly as the keeping-room.

We had a beautiful double wedding in the summer, in our old church, and since that I have come to make the old Hall homelike to my boy in the holidays.

We are very happy together when he comes home, and fills the house with his young friends; and if it feels too large and empty for me in his absence, I can always walk down for a happy afternoon with Emily, or go and make a longer visit to Jaquetta.

And I don't think, as a leader of the fashion, she would have been half so happy as the motherly, active, ready-handed doctor's wife.

But best of all to me, are those quiet moments when Alured's earnest spirit shows itself, and he talks out what is in his heart; that it is a great responsibility to stand in the place such a man as Fulk would have had—yes —and to have been saved at the cost of Trevor's life.

I believe the pure, calm remembrance of Trevor Lea's life will be his guiding star, and that he will be worthy of it.